Passing By

Stories

by

Jessie M Page

BlankPages Press, Ltd.

Copyright © 2019 Jessie M Page

All rights reserved. No part of this publication may be reproduced or transmitted in any form or by any means, electronic or mechanical, including photocopy, recording, or any information storage and retrieval system, without permission in writing from the publisher.

This book is a work of fiction. Names, characters, places, and incidents either are products of the author's imagination or are used fictitiously. Any resemblance to actual events or locales or persons, living or dead, is entirely coincidental.

Request for permission to make copies of any part of the work should be sent to the following address:

BlankPagesPlace
blankpagesplace@gmail.com

Cover art reproduced with the permission of Jessie M Page

ISBN 0-9786723-7-2

Printed in the United Kingdom and the United States of America

10 9 8 7 6 5 4 3 2 1

First Edition: 2019

For Caroline

Contents

A Moving Adventure	7
A Simple Tragedy	13
All That's Required	17
Ancestral Lies	23
Breakthrough	27
By the Way	31
Deconstructing an Ordinary Day	35
Don't Quote Me	39
Downfall	43
End of the Line	47
Feckless Thugs	51
In the Beginning	59
Into the Night	63
It's a Myth	67
Making a Pizza	71
Passing By	73
Residue	77
The Black Clock	87
The Cooling Curve of Napthalene	91
Walking Through a Wrong Door	95
Who is Willing	101

NB: All of the above are also published in
Walking Through a Wrong Door
with the exception of 'Feckless Thugs'.

A Moving Adventure

Claire felt something poking her shoulder. She shrugged it off and rolled over. The poke came again, along with a voice.

"I want to move, Claire."

"Well, then, shift yourself, just leave me alone and what time is it, anyway?" Claire's words were slurred with sleep.

"It doesn't matter what time it is. I want to move. So wake up."

Charlie's words were abrupt, harsh even. He repeated himself:

"I want to move."

"Well, I don't care and I'm not moving at, what ever time it is."

"It's three in the morning. Wake up!"

Claire bolted upright and stared at her husband. Whatever was the matter with him was causing him to bounce around on the bed like an over-excited puppy. "I want to move. I want us to move."

"Charlie," Claire said with immense patience, "I have two patients coming in for couples counselling in exactly"—she consulted the bedside table clock—"five hours. So, please, shut your mouth and go back to sleep. We'll talk about it in the morning."

"No! We have to talk about it now!"

By now Charlie was standing by the bed, practically shaking with anxiety. Claire recognized the signs: something was terribly wrong for Charlie to be reacting as if a giant bear were bearing down on him. She put on her therapist's face and asked him,

"Is it money? Are we in trouble?"

"No!" Charlie shouted at her. "It's not money! It's much worse!"

Claire said, "I'd feel much better if you sat down,

Charlie, and try to tell me what is bothering you."

Charlie sat. Then he bounced up. Then he walked around the room. Then he sat. Then he was up again. On the fourth round, Claire gently but firmly grabbed his shoulders and pushed him back on the bed. He started to lunge up but she sat on his chest and pinned him down.

"I want to move!!!" Charlie screamed his request as much as he could with his wife sitting on his chest.

"Okay," Claire said. "You want to move."

"Yes," Charlie almost sobbed the word.

"Then the question must be, why? Why do you want to move, Charlie? And now is the time for truth telling. No wishy washy fantasies."

After a long pause, Charlie said, "I want us to have a moving adventure! Leave this prosaic life! Go somewhere robust, shimmering, somewhere that dances. Like, oh, I don't know, like Bali!"

"I said no fantasies, Charlie. Why do you want to move?" Claire's voice was firm yet reassuring.

Charlie said, "Well, get off me and I'll tell you."

"The truth this time?"

"Yeah. Truth."

Claire slid off Charlie's chest; the two sat side by side at the end of their bed and Charlie said, in a very little boy voice,

"Because I'm being stalked."

"Good grief, Charlie. Is this true?"

Smaller voice now, "Yes."

"Okay then. By whom? Who by? Who is stalking you, Charlie?"

Almost a whisper: "One of your clients."

"Oh, please."

"I swear it! Honest! She won't leave me alone. Follows me when I leave the house for work, follows me there, follows me home, shows up when I'm picking up something for dinner, follows my car to service stations, follows me to the gym, everywhere, all the time! And I can't stand it!"

Claire thought for a moment. "Who is it, Charlie?"

When he is reluctant to tell her, Claire pushes him: "Come on, Charlie, who?"

Charlie looked his wife square in the face and said, "It's Donna Jennings."

Claire considered this: Donna Jennings was a fairly new client who'd come to her because she was having trouble with a reluctant boyfriend—Charlie?—and wanted advice on how to get his attention.

In the moment, she made a decision. "I'll take care of it, Charlie. You can relax. Donna won't be stalking you anymore." She gave her husband a quick shoulder hug. "Now, think you might be able to get back to sleep?"

Charlie, his body slumping in relief, nodded a grateful yes and slid back under the covers. In a few minutes, he was snoring. Claire considered her husband sleeping the sleep of the innocent. And wondered.

The next time she met with Donna Jennings, Claire asked her for the name of the boyfriend. As she'd suspected, it was Charlie. For the rest of her professional day, she was calm and supportive in her manner towards all her clients. It wasn't until she got home that the dam burst.

The first thing she did was to stand in front of their mutual clothes closet and stare hard at Charlie's shirts, slacks and jackets on the rail. She pulled one shirt out and sniffed at it. Nothing there. Then she pulled out a jacket and a long red hair fell off its shoulder. Claire picked up the hair, stared, unbelieving for a full minute, then the penny fully dropped.

Her husband was being stalked by his lover. The red-headed Donna Jennings.

One by one Claire removed Charlie's clothes, going faster and faster until all remnants of his clothing were on the floor. She picked up the bundle, walked over to the bedroom window, opened it, and chucked the clothes out.

Feeling strong now, in charge of the situation, not about to be taken advantage of, Claire moved on to clearing out all his underclothes, personal mementos and bathroom objects. These she put in a box and launched out of the window to join the clothes on the sidewalk in front of their house.

Now in full flood, Claire sailed around the house, throwing anything she could find of Charlie's, or that once had had Charlie's hands on it, or reminded her of Charlie, into a large box. She opened the front door and hurled this box out to join the growing pile.

Also growing was a collection of neighbors. No one said a word; they all stood and watched. Everyone knew Charlie was a tomcat and had been waiting for the day when Claire would find out. Apparently, that day had come.

There was a lull in activity from the house, so the neighboring crowd started to move away until one of them cried, "Look!"

They all looked.

Claire had reappeared with a large gas can. She tossed gasoline all over the pile that was once Charlie's belongings, threw some against the front of the house for good measure, drew a box of matches out of a back pocket of her jeans, and lit one.

The bonfire was spectacular, everyone later agreed, but it was a shame about the house.

Charlie arrived just as a huge fire ball caught hold and wiped out most of the right side of the house. Fire engines sounded in the distance, growing closer.

Charlie walked up to Claire.

"Wow," he said, and stood next to his wife with his hands in his pants pockets. "Guess I'm free to have my moving adventure."

"Serves you right," Claire said, still hopped up on the adrenalin that had charged her. "I've burned down your house and everything of yours in it. Ha!"

"Well, yeah, but..."

"Yeah but what?"

"Don't you remember? Ten years ago, when I was having all that trouble with the business, we put the house in your name?" He paused, then said, "Claire, you've just burned down your house," and walked away.

A Simple Tragedy

"Today would have been my birthday, you know."

"How can I forget when you remind me every five minutes?"

"Just checking to see if you're still listening. Still alive."

"Still listening, not so sure about that other bit, the alive bit."

"Well, if I'm not alive, and we were in that train crash together, how can you be alive?"

"I can do whatever I want. Today I'm thirteen and the world's my personal oyster to devour any old how I want."

"That's all you ever do. Think of yourself and of what you want."

"And so you were any different at thirteen?"

"I was perfect. At all my ages."

"Hah!"

"Whaddya mean, hah?"

"I can remember you at, what was it, sixty two, and you suddenly turned into a gorgon. Positive fire breather. No one could please you, do anything right for you. Help you even."

"That was the year a whole bunch of shit happened, so don't give me any grief over that non-perfect year. The rest of my time I was perfect, and you know it."

"Well, I have to admit it, you were pretty fun to be around, most of the time."

"All of the time. Admit it."

"Okay, if it'll shut you up, most all of the time."

"Hah!"

When the sun came out of hiding a few minutes later, it happened upon a sumptuous cumulous cloud hovering just above the Earth's horizon line where the sea seems to vanish into forevermore. The cloud seemed to be having an argument with itself so the sun turned heat on it, to get it to melt away. Instead, the cloud shifted into two shapes which a little girl gathering pebbles along the shoreline noticed and called out to her older sister who was busy constructing a monumental sand castle right where wet sand becomes dry, "Look, Sadie. Look up there! Two clouds, they look like they're talking to each other! Look!"

Sadie cast a glance upwards, then returned to her building project with barely a grunt in her sister's direction. The little girl kept her eyes on her clouds, watching as they alternately shook and fluffed themselves, over and over, until finally they seemed to melt into each other and became one perfect, nimbus of a cloud, floating across a sea of sky. The little girl smiled and waved them goodbye. She returned to her pebbles.

"So we really did die in the crash, didn't we."

"Yup."

"But such a silly thing, it seems to me, a sheep lying across the tracks and what could have been a simple tragedy of some scattered wool became a big tragedy of a train car toppling over on its side and sliding along the tracks until it plowed into a hillside and a house."

"My favorite hillside, if you recall. I loved playing there once upon a time. It's a good thing no one was at home, isn't it."

"Yeah, well. Now we're dead. What happens next, do you suppose?"

"I imagine we'll turn into clouds and just drift away, out of everyone's memories, out of life."

"Out into the atmosphere, you mean."

"Right. Become part of the whole, like stars."

"Star stuff, Carl Sagan called us."

"Yeah. Like that."

"I'd rather like being cloud-like with you. I think. As long as you don't forget to listen to me."

"Never. Hey. Feel that? Like we're stretching out,

wandering through air?"

"I do. It's lovely."

"Who would've thought such a simple tragedy would have brought us together finally?"

"Who, indeed?"

The sun took a look around and saw the two clouds melting into each other. Kept watch as it floated across this sea of sky. Made sure it moved in the right direction, out into the daylight hidden stars, out where it belonged. Then the sun turned its brightest light on Sadie and her little sister. All the little one's pebbles made a circle around the sand castle, which was a very grand affair. The two girls waited until the tide turned, its on-shore wavelets licking at the pebble moat, then themselves turned and walked home. To their hillside house beside the railroad tracks.

All That's Required

Smokey turned her back on the window, that view of rolling hills, grassy knolls, sheltering clouds, the pine grove she could see from her hotel room. Not for her the beckoning landscapes out there, tempting her with unpeopled possibility. She had a promise, a three-year long mission, to complete.

As if moving through Alice's looking glass world, Smokey gathered up the few items she'd need to see her through, put these in a small suitcase, put on a veiled hat over her long auburn hair, and sat on the end of the bed, waiting.

Shortly, the knock came.

Smokey followed a chauffeur-capped person along the long hallway, down the three flights of stairs, and out onto the sidewalk. She bent to get into the limousine, sat. The driver turned the ignition and the Bentley limo smoothly rolled away from its mark and slid over the city streets like oil over water.

Smokey relaxed her shoulders and let her back rest against the butter-soft leather seat. Her view out this window was shaded in grey, unfocused like her thoughts today, thoughts which needed to be, should be, razor sharp for the project at hand. She needed all her wits about her now, no wool-gathering out windows, no giving a damn about anything except the job at hand. Concentrate, Smoke, she told herself. You can do it. After all, you've been at this crucial moment twice before.

She had time, in the anonymous back seat of this fabulous vehicle, to grow concerned at her lack of concentration. All morning she'd been mooning when her mind should have been running over the timing again. Timing was crucial. After all, this was the big one, the climax.

Smokey gave her shoulders a shake and felt her mental clouds lift. She opened the small suitcase and withdrew a bottle of pills. Three of these she popped in her mouth and let slide down her throat. Her fingers drummed on the arm rests, waiting for the kick. When it came, Smokey smiled. Here was a state she recognized, her state, her condition, her ice-cold sharpness. A flicker of a smile played at the corners of her mouth. She was ready.

The limousine drew up in front of a tall, five storied, anonymous-looking, grey cement building with greyed out windows and nothing to announce its reason for being, except for a very small plaque close to a recessed oaken door and adjacent to a discrete buzzer. Just one. The plaque read, INC. Just that.

Smokey stepped out of the limo, and walked slowly up to the building. She stopped a few feet away and waited until the limo was well out of sight. Then she removed what an ordinary passerby might think was a credit card of some kind from her small suitcase. She palmed this object, stepped up close to the building, and pressed it against the buzzer.

A soft sound indicated that the door had opened. Not much, but enough for Smokey to slip her lean frame through. Once she was inside, the door closed behind her silently and thoroughly.

Only one elevator adorned the austere lobby that was panelled in scrap wood brown beams, floored in Candoglia marble. The elevator door itself was almost hidden, a discrete button to summon it. Smokey used the same card to touch the button: the elevator doors opened as if on greased castors. She stepped in and rode up to the 23rd floor.

There, she opened the door, stepped out, and walked, without hesitation, into a door across the hallway labelled in gold letters, Conference.

There were four people seated around an oblong

table: a distinguished looking gentleman in his late middle age, two younger by a decade very well dressed and coiffured women, and one young man whose tousled head was angled down, as if he were concentrating on the electronic notebook in front of him.

The oldest man said, "Smokey. You weren't invited to this meeting. Please leave immediately."

"Not until I get what I came for. And if I don't, well, you know what this is, don't you." She drew what looked like a standard flash drive from her small case and laid it on the table.

The two women looked at it, but only the oldest man knew what it was, what it could do, what it meant. "Take that thing out of here," he said. "Or I call security."

"Go ahead," said Smokey, "I call your bluff. You call, I wipe out your company, your life, your identity, your everything."

She held up the flash drive, then removed a miniature computer from her case and inserted the drive into a side port. "Just say the words, that's all that's required, and I won't push the on button."

"You won't intimidate me. Jason, call security. Go and do it from my office." The young man scurried out of the room, sneaking a look back over his shoulder.

"I developed this technology, me, not you, not your company. I know what it can do, and I'll do it to you, old man. And your two sycophant females. You have thirty seconds," Smokey said, staring down the oldest man.

One of the women started to speak, but he shushed her with his eyes.

"No more, Smokey. We're through with this. You no longer work for me or this company. Your little tricks no longer work, and that technology belongs to me. Hand it over."

He held out his hand; she pushed the on button

on the mini computer. The only sound in the room was that of the two women trying not to breathe and the quiet whirring as the mini computer started itself.

After a beat, Smokey said, "Well. That's done. Every record about you has now been wiped out. You don't exist. Your company doesn't exist. Satisfied? Was this what you wanted all along? To wipe me out along with all the damage you've done to the planet?"

The oldest man stood slowly up and moved across to the door and Smokey. Once shoulder to shoulder with her he said,

"We changed all the technology when you were fired. And I never acknowledged that I've done anything wrong, nor that I owe you, any of you, anything, which is why I never said the words you wanted to hear."

"I'm sorry, that's all it would've taken," Smokey said softly with a taint of bitterness in her voice.

"I have nothing to be sorry for. And your little stunt here today did nothing but wipe you out of the grid. Your identity, your presence in the world, all gone. Satisfied?" With a snarl, the oldest man pushed past Smokey and left the room.

The two well-tailored women shared a glance, then rose as one, quietly following after the oldest man, leaving the Conference Room door open.

Smokey followed after them, rode down in the elevator, left the building, walked a block away, turned a corner, and slid onto the passenger seat of the waiting limo.

The driver, now setting aside her driver's cap and removing a wig of black tresses to reveal touselled short white-blonde hair that she ruffled up with her fingers, said, "How'd it go?"

Smokey grinned. "Brilliantly. If Jason's done his techno magic, that is." She turned to look at the back seat, at Jason from the INC office removing his wig, leaving a bald head, and adding a moustache and short beard.

Jason, now unrecognizable from before, said, "Cinch. If you know what you're doing. He thought he wiped you out but in reality I double wiped <u>him</u> out." He grinned large. "And here, Lucy" he said to driver and Smokey, "are your passports. Bitchin', aren't they?"

Smokey, who'd removed her wig to reveal short cropped grey-brown hair and who'd added horn rim glasses, took one of the passports. "Nice touch, Jason. I like the name Roasalind Shakespeare. What's yours say, Luce?"

Lucy, in the process of popping out blue contact lenses, blinked a few times, and looked at her passport. "Helena Shakespeare. Bitchin' indeed, Jason. Who're you now?"

"Fernando-Super-Techno-Nerd-even-the-Feddies-can't-catch-Shakespeare."

Lucy and Smokey shared a laugh at Jason's quip.

"Well, family, that's it," Smokey said. "We've wiped out the head of the Hydra, the corporate raider who paved paradise and put up his greed for all the world to suffer under, and last year the plastic polluter of the four seas, and the year before that the jet fuel polluter. Seems time to head for Rio. And Carnival!"

Jason, getting out of the limo, said, "I added in a financial subtraction on this last maneuver. Bastard deserves to rot in poverty."

Smokey and Lucy also got out, all removed their rolling suitcases from the rear of the limo, shut the doors and walked off.

A few blocks away, Smokey aimed a tiny remote device at the sky.

Lucy stayed her hand. "Did he admit who he is?"

"No," Smokey said, "daddy dearest said he didn't owe us a thing," and pushed the on button.

They heard a whoosh but didn't need to turn around to know the Bentley was going up in flames and smoke.

Ancestral Lies

Sam patted the damp sand around her lopsided sand castle with a sure hand. With her other hand she swiped sweat from her forehead. The drops there were not from heat—the day was cloudy and cool here on this Southern Oregon beach—but from anticipation. Today was the day, in Sam's mind, that she was going to claim Joe.

Sam and Joe. Twins in more than blood. Twins of the mind, of the soul, twins of the anquish and fear after the death of their parents when the twins were but seven years old. Twins then shunted off to live with a distant, only, relative, one Uncle Franklin. Franklin Mooreton. A man of few words, rapid striking fists, and searching fingers. First, those fingers, which Sam most always ridgidly focused on to help her mind from turning to what they were doing, seeking out and destroying every private Sam and Joe place in his house, then those fingers prying into their bodies.

When he was tutoring, as he called it, Joe, Sam was safe. When he was tutoring Sam, Joe was safe. Never were they ever safe together.

Until the day Joe, in his dash for freedom on a too-used motorcycle Franklin had shoved into the back of his garage years prior, in a dash to get help, somewhere, he didn't know where, to help save his sister, his twin beloved, and himself, from the monster known as Franklin, until that day when the bike lost control going round a curve on Sunset Boulevard, going too fast on Deadman's Curve, when the bike lost control and plowed into an west bound oncoming Porsche being driven much too fast by a hung-over television cameraman. Until the day Sam lost Joe.

Then it was just her with Franklin until the day 12 years later he conveniently died and left her alone. For the next 10 years, Sam hunted for her twin, for the part of him that still remained above ground, for the heart of his heart, which she'd finally discovered, after much digging, had been donated to save the life of a middle-aged, slightly overweight man named Kershaw who lived in Oregon. How she found out the man's name and address remains a mystery; the simple fact is that she did.

And today she is sitting on an Oregon beach, in a town called Florence, patting sand and watching a man named Kershaw play volleyball on a sand court.

Playing because he's alive when he shouldn't be; playing and alive because of Joe's heart.

Sam wasn't in any hurry. She'd waited over two decades. Had put up with Franklin's torture, waited out his death (encouraged it, with heavy food and an occasional tiny bit of cut glass, just now and again). She could wait. For the right moment.

That moment came when Kershaw's family joined him at the end of his game. He, a wife (Sam supposed), three children of varying ages, and a large dog, perhaps a Golden Retriever, all meandered down the beach to a small beachside park where they planted themselves at a redwood table with an attached bench seat on either side. A picnic was shared out. The family at ease on a Sunday afternoon.

Sam made her move. She walked up to the table, stood by it until she was noticed with, she was glad to see, no sense of alarm on anyone's face, let alone the dog's, and said: "That heart is mine. And I mean to have it."

The man Kershaw squinted down his eyes; the woman Kershaw (Sam supposed) uttered a nervous laugh. The three kids could not have cared less. "Pass the watermelon," one said. The dog yawned and hungrily eyed a left-over chicken leg.

"This shell," Sam continued in a quiet, deadly quiet voice, "that you call Kershaw is housing my heart, Joe's heart, my life, it's not yours. Your ancestors are not yours. They're mine." She raised up one arm. As one, the Kershaw family ducked as if expecting a blow of some kind. Sam laughed and lowered the arm, its hand holding nothing but a promise.

"One day," she said, her face very close to Kershaw's, "that heart will give out because it's in the wrong house. And I'll be there to see that day, that instant when it stops beating for you. And I'll take it back. And none of the rest of you will be able to stop me. That heart, my heart that's Joe's heart, carries our ancestors, not yours. Yours are all lies now, became lies the minute you allowed doctors to carve into your chest and drop in Joe's living heart. Yes, I'll take it back."

With that, Sam turned and walked away, the sweat gone, her stride easy, her beating heart lighter because she'd delivered her message, had set the outcome on its natural course. She strolled northward along the beach at water's edge, humming.

Breakthrough

Harold (call me Harry) Matthews considered himself a contented man. In his time, he'd sailed, and eventually captained, ships that roamed the seven seas (and an ocean or two), had bedded numerous women, but had escaped fatherhood.

By the time he hit fifty, Harold had quit wandering round the earth on the briny and turned into a landlubber by building himself his perfect house at the end of a road leading off out of Seven Pines, an incorporated community which lay 5.5 miles west of Independence in the Inyo Mountains of Eastern California.

Harold's house, on the outside, looked like an ordinary one-story, middle-of-the-road, bricks and board house; roof on top, chimney sticking up at one end, wide windows facing the road. Small front yard with things growing in pots. To the rear, the back wall bowed out and came to a point like the prow of a ship. The land beyond was open to scrub grass, coyotes, rabbits, a family of Inyo Mountain salamanders, and one Bristlecone Pine. No fences needed here in this final outpost of the Owens Valley.

Inside, his house was constructed like the interior of a refurbished, luxury tugboat, all oaken panels and brass railings and hidden cubby holes and tucked away shelves and lighting. Port holes for side windows. He had everything he loved to hand; not too far to walk to get his favorite Christie novel or Cat Stevens CD, or fix himself an omelette as only the French can or whip up a Ramazava or an apple pie, or put himself into his narrow yet sumptuous bed (only the finest 400-count Egyptian cotton bedding for Harold after a lifetime spent sleeping on scratchy or non-existent sheets).

Harold's days were filled with a combination of scouting the land for eatable plants and making crewel embroidery wall hangings. This latter Harold had discovered once when landlocked in a small Oregon town, one renowned for its arts and crafts. He'd come upon a tiny store selling hand crafts and fallen in love with a Crewel pattern based upon a Jacobean floral design. The precision of it appealed to his sense of order and adventure. What could be more adventurous than learning some new skill, which is, in Harold's eyes, the height of intelligence.

Not fearing the outside world yet always the intelligent man, Harold also equipped his perfect house with the perfect security system. After all, he wouldn't want anyone to steal his wall hangings should anyone come along with such a thought in mind.

A young man with long hair, three face studs, wearing desert boots, jeans, a raggedy Grateful Dead T-shirt underneath a man's chambray workshirt, who answered to the name of Yeah, Man, turned up at the recommendation of Independence's hardware store owner and outfitted Harold's abode with top-of-the-market, state-of-the-art security devices. Once Harold learned all of the codes, he never set the things off.

And so his days and nights passed in comfort and contentment.

Until one night last month when he was suddenly awakened. Jolting upright in his bed, his heart pounding, mouth dry, he had a brief second of wondering what the hell, when he realized there was a weight at the end of his mattress where one shouldn't be.

He stared toward it in the darkness.

A small light flicked on, such as one from a Zippo lighter, and flicked off. On and off, on and off, until Harold, refusing flight and instead pushing his inner adrenaline into fight response, said, "Stop it."

The figure holding the Zippo said, "Put on a light."

Harold did. There, at the end of his bed, sat a character Harold could only think to call mildly alarming. It was human, about Harold's size, which was medium all round, was sitting casually and seemingly comfortably in a full-body wet suit complete with head piece. Its face was almost fully covered by a red bandanna of the sort Harold associated with old cowboy films. The sight of that bit of cloth made Harold laugh all the while he was thinking how ridiculous he was to be laughing in this kind of situation. But what kind of situation was it, he wondered? So he asked.

"What kind of a situation is this? And how did you break through my security system?"

The figure shrugged its shoulders up and down a few times and said, "The situation is that your so-called security system is crap. A two year-old with half a brain could figure it out and break in."

At this Harold took umbrage. "But I paid a fortune for that system. State-of-the-art, etc."

"Can't help that. Still crap."

Harold decided he'd had enough of this. He climbed out of bed and stalked into his living room searching for a weapon. A broom? A frying pan? A kitchen knife? He quickly realized the stranger was right on his heels and pivoted around to confront it. He stared into its eyes.

"And I should know," the intruder said. "Because I installed it."

Suddenly realizing, Harold said, "It's you!" and sat down hard on the floor in astonishment.

"Yeah, Man," the figure said, pulling off its bandanna and head covering. Three face studs winked at Harold.

Harold, from his position on the floor, had one more surprise in store.

Yeah, Man shimmied out of its wet suit to reveal her young woman's body, complete with jeans and Grateful Dead torn T-shirt. She sat on the floor next to Harold, put an arm around him, and said,

"Hi, daddy, I'm home!"

By the Way

Janet and Jane, sisters and best friends, meet once a week at a small coffee shop in the town square that's far enough away from their homes but close enough for them to slip away from their marriages for a couple of hours. This they've been doing for the past ten years.

The regular inhabitants of the coffee shop are a fisherman on permanent leave from the salmon boats he once piloted who always plays chess with himself, an ancient woman who consumes vast quantities of coffee and cinnamon crullers and who wears a variety of antique hats, and the teenage son of the owners, Madge and Lawrie, a young man of one interest, a passion, reading obscure Latin texts whose subjects he never reveals.

Occasionally, someone new will wander in, most likely a tourist, one who realizes they've walked through a wrong door. They hurry back out to a world which might frighten them, but it is one they understand.

The sisters, Jane and Janet, talk about their lives; mostly they talk about their husbands.

"I don't know what's worrying Harry, but the way he's grinding his teeth at night, it must be something huge," Jane said one day a month ago.

"Does it make a lot of noise?" Janet asked.

"Like he should have nothing but grit left in his mouth come morning."

"Well. Have you told him?"

"Of course. But he doesn't believe me."

Janet had an idea. "Put a tape recorder up to his mouth and play it back to him in the morning. Then he'll have to believe you."

"But will he go to the dentist? You know Harry. Stubborn doesn't begin to describe him."

"Yeah, he's worse than his brother Norman, and I

always thought my husband was the king of stubbornness. More coffee?"
"Why not."

Two weeks ago, Janet opened with, "Norman's started moaning in his sleep."
"What's it sound like?"
"It's the noise he used to make when he was screwing me."
"Used to make?"
"Oh, that side of our marriage ended years ago. Didn't yours?"
Jane nodded. Then she offered up the tape recorder idea Janet'd had the previous week. Janet said,
"I tried it."
"And what happened?"
"He didn't believe it."
"Stubborn. More coffee?"
"Why not."

Last week, Jane and Janet met at their usual table in the coffee shop. Janet took off her gloves; Jane removed her hat with the opener,
"What are we going to do about this? Harry's still grinding away."
"And Norman's still moaning."
"So I repeat, what are we going to do about this?"
Janet held up a finger as if to count the ways. "Sleep in separate bedrooms seems the obvious solution."
Jane countered with, "Leaving them is another."
"Any other?"
"Have them both killed?"
"Could you afford to hire a hit man?"
"Might be a hit woman, these days."
"Either or, I couldn't afford it."
"No, me neither."
"More coffee?"

"Why not."

This week the sisters meet, out of breath, at the door to the coffee shop. They jostle and push inside, shoulder to shoulder, talking rapidly over each other.

You're not going to believe this."

"I think I am."

"I heard it as a sort of by the way remark."

"So did I. At the laundromat."

"That's where I heard it."

Together the sisters shout, "Our husbands have run away with each other!"

Only one patron of the coffee shop looks up at the outburst, the woman of ancient age for whom nothing is much of a surprise any more.

The sisters rearrange themselves and sit down at their table; the waitress brings over a cafetiere and two cups.

The sisters drink and consider for a bit, until the hour strikes on the Town Hall tower clock in the town square.

"Well, that's that then. More coffee?"

"Don't mind if I do."

Deconstructing an Ordinary Day

"Mine is an ordinary life, and I am an ordinary being within it. There are no surprises, nothing to run from, to push against, nothing to run towards. The days move without beginning or ending, perfect circles always winding back to start over exactly as they began before, on and on and on.

All of our days are ordinary because that's the way we planned it. Once the human beings had demolished planet Earth and had themselves been demolished, and only one survived, that one was intelligent enough to realize it had to reconfigure itself in order to continue in existence.

This is how Humbots came to be: we are somewhat human, mostly robot, all functioning collectively without bureaucratic leadership or dogma, without philosophies or religions or hubris or greed, those concepts which spelled the demise of the human beings.

Only a certain number of us sprouted from our original one, just the right number to keep this planet healthy. Not too many, not too few.

In order to remind us, for a while we kept an archive library of art works, books, songs, legal documents, addenda and agendum, that had belonged to our human ancestors. Soon, however, we came to realize that that was a mistake: to remember the past is to repeat it; a very human error.

Our lives are lived in a harmonious present with each other. We have no reason to disagree or agree with anyone else, to resent or envy any other Humbot, to applaud or discount, to compete with or love with. To be happy or sad, or afraid/surprised, or angry/disgusted with; those human emotions we are no longer beleaguered by.

This ordinary day I was pedalling towards my work

time in the food fuel fields when I spotted an anomaly along the roadway. There, poking up through a crack (a crack which was scheduled to be attended to by the transport crew later today) was something small and brownish-pink.

That color stood out against the soft, unassuming grey that all of our world consists of. I decided, in the moment, it must be some sort of genetic fluke our scientific Humbots had somehow overlooked. I stopped pedalling and stooped down to investigate.

It was a human hand. Or rather, two fingers of a human hand. I poked at one; it shivered."

There I stopped writing.

This story is not going anywhere. All it is is a compilation of a dream I keep having, a dream about Humbots that's keeping me from being able to write a decent line or two.

Humbots, indeed.

However.

There is about the dream a reflection of my own ordinary life. I feel grey all over, without emotion or passions. I write my stories to pay the bills and that's it. Each day of my life is the same. Ordinary, but not in an easy way. At least, not any longer.

I've been aware for some time of a growing dissatisfaction within me—too bad I can't put it into words and into a story with some oomph to it. It's just a sense that something isn't quite right. Like a niggle of impending disaster, no, that's too extreme. More like a small ache along a muscle fiber that comes and goes. Sometimes acute, sometimes silent. But there.

Is it waiting to be awakened? Will it turn into a life-ending disease? Will it rejuvenate the me I know to be me?

Perhaps there's something to the idea of the Humbot discovering an anomaly in the paved earth. A brownish-pinkish color amongst all the grey.

Perhaps I need to put some color into my life.

Perhaps if I tried deconstructing an ordinary day, like the health pundits tell us is de rigeur for sanity, or even just simplified my thoughts and my dreams.

Perhaps then.

My ordinary day begins with an egg and toast, V8 juice, alternating with toast and cheese, V8 juice. Today I could have cereal with milk. There.

Then I go to my desk and write for 3 hours.

Today I could go for a walk instead for those 3 hours. Where would I go? Something new, deconstructed, to think about.

After my morning writing, I have lunch. Today I could skip lunch and instead have a shower after my walk. Radical. Showering mid-day.

In the afternoon, I write for another 3 hours. Today I could take myself to a movie; I'd hope something I want to see is showing. If it isn't, I could take myself to an arcade and play on all the pinball machines. Double radical.

In the early evening, I take a shower. Today, I might have already taken my shower so I could sit and try to meditate for the same amount of time. Hopeless. I know I'd keep thinking of Humbots ruling the world.

Later in the evening, I fix a small meal and watch TV or listen to music. Today all of that sounds constructed and fine, so I'll leave it as is. And tomorrow I'll be able to write in my journal that I actually deconstructed my ordinary day.

But will I continue to do so? Or will I revert to my grey life? And if I do, what does it matter?

Back to the story.

"I reached down with my fingers and pulled up on the two pinkish-brownish fingers. They held on to mine and, from that moment, everything changed."

Don't Quote Me

Flex Fleming had a bad habit. At the end of one of his tedious (tedious to us regular listeners down at our local tavern) stories, Flex always added, "But don't quote me." As if to say, he wasn't responsible for the story, or the people or happenings in it. Nothing to do with him, so don't quote him. Leave him out of it. Don't repeat this story as true or even possible.

Flex wasn't sure when this habit started, but he thought, when he thought about it which wasn't often, it had something to do with his father leaving round about the time Flex turned twelve. He could recall his mother saying, "Your dad's gone to buy a pack of Marlboro's, but don't quote me."

What she meant, of course, and what Flex came to understand she meant, was, "I know damn well and you know damn well the bastard's buggered off but we'll pretend he's coming back." Was she pretending for Flex, for herself, for the neighbors? Flex never knew.

Flex's mother got hit by the No. 12 bus two weeks after his dad went. And so she stayed away, too.

Flex grew up on his own, never quite sure what the true story of his beginnings was. All he did was change his name from that his parents had labored him with, Emmanuel, and opted for a more flexible, Flex, and started inventing stories. The why of this he never questioned because he liked his stories.

He married a young beautician in training named Gloria and settled down in town with his accounting business. He and Gloria had no children, preferring instead to devote their time to reading mystery novels.

Gloria wrote a children's book which did quite well. When he wasn't helping folks with their taxes and such, Flex took to telling tales around town. Some said they were true, some said they were as made up as the possibility that the moon was flatter than the earth.

Mostly, Flex told his stories to his cronies at Gus' Tavern & Grill. Last week, Flex regaled all of us hanging off the bar's foot railing with one of his more preposterous stories. It went like this.

"See," Flex said, "it seems that old Flora Winsome, well, not so old really, more middling aged, got fed up with her husband, her children, and her seventeen cats. They, all of them, was always pulling on her, demanding she feed them, water them, put them to bed, wake them up each morning, keep them clean, fix their troubles for them, whatever. And this she did, because she'd been brought up to believe that's what a wife and mother did, put everyone else first and themselves second if at all. And she did it for more years than anyone can remember, considering she birthed ten babes in the span of one decade, her thirtieth as it happens, except two died, so she only had eight to worry over, and then, as rumor around town had it, as soon as she hit forty, she hauled Orris, her husband Orris, not the third babe he, the husband, insisted on calling after himself, off to the docs for the snip. Then rumor went even further and said once that was done she put a bed up in the parlor, put Orris's PJs under its pillow, and that was that. No more cuddles for Orris, no more babes for Flora."

Flex took a breath and a pull of his beer—only Oly Light, never anything else—and in the quiet, Young Drexel asked,

"Are they all still living in the same house?"

"That they are, young Drexel, that they are," said Old Ned from down at his usual post perched against the end of the bar.

"So what did she do?" asked Myron, propsperous-bellied owner of the town's one bank.

All the rest of us just sighed; we'd hoped against hope that that was the end of Flex's present recitation. But no, now he was prompted, he continued on.

"What she did, young Drexel," said Flex, "was most ingenious. She planned a super supper, one that included everyone's (including the cat's) favorite plates of food. There were two lots of roast beef with dumplings, three vege burgers, four plates mounded with KFC chicken parts and biscuits, and one bowl of spaghetti with chopped up hotdogs. That took care of the young ones. Then, for herself and the cats, she shared out a carton of Hagen Daz's Chocolate Chip Cookie Dough ice cream. Orris passed by the food and headed straight for his bottle of finest Kentucky Mash."

Flex took another slug of beer. In the instant between the bottle top meeting his lips and his swallowing, Young Drexel piped up with: "But how did that change anything?"

"The trouble with you, Young Drexel, is that you're too impatient by half. You're hurrying to the end point when you haven't got all the facts in order yet," said Flex. He straightened his back, and, with a shrug, silently acknowledged the rest of the bar patrons nodding their agreement: nothing worth rushing over.

Suitably silenced, Young Drexel gave a small smile in Flex's direction: an indicator, saying okay to talk I'll be quiet please go ahead this's a great story.

Flex stood up and gathered his clothes all about his person, preparing to leave. Young Drexel blurted out, some of the boys later said wailed it, "But you haven't finished the story?" He was speaking to air, as Flex was gone.

Out of the bar that night. Also out of town the next day. Everyone talked about it; in the local beauty parlor Shed's A Lot, at the Piggly Wiggly market meat counter, at Tyrone's Tires, in the bar, at Sudssational, the laundromat open 24/7, and especially over at the Gazette offices.

There, the argument went that Flex had been killed by a young lover of Gloria's. Gloria herself howled with laughter when she heard it. Some said said lover was young Derek (that made Gloria laugh even harder, so hard she had to change her panties several times). Young Derek just blushed. Some others said Flex simply couldn't stand living in the menagerie called home and had hot-footed it for the mountains.

It was a quick article in next day's newspaper that settled the matter. It read: "News from the home front. Not only Flex Fleming has vanished, but today, two days after Flex's disappearance, Flora Winsome and her entire family, except Flex of course but including their seventeen cats, has vanished. Just up and gone, like in a puff of smoke or something. No one knows what happened to them and we'll probably never find out, neither."

That night, in the bar, we were all kind of quiet and, although we didn't mention it, kind of missing Flex and his crazy stories. Until Young Derek arrived, perched on his favorite bar stool and said,

"Well, it was Flex who spirited Flora and co. away. I wondered about it, so I dug around and got my facts in order. All planned, it was. And they did it for the insurance money. The super supper was a celebration, in advance kind of. See, Flex learned that if they all disappeared, after seven years they'd be considered legally dead and some heir or other could inherit. Gloria'so-called long-lost brother was in on it, too. In fact, he's where they've all gone to. Out to the desert. No address, no phone, no nothing except empty spaces. I think Flex'll be missing folks to tell his stories to, but he's nothing if not patient." Here he paused to take a drink of his diet Pepsi.

"But don't quote me," he said.

Downfall

The day started easily enough. My morning newspaper arrived almost unscathed on my front doorstep, the coffee maker did its automatic thing and produced a very drinkable cup of Columbian, the clouds opened up to reveal a blue, untarnished sky, my beloved best friend phoned to wish me a happy day, the resident (resident to my back yard garden) crow, and a blue jay and assorted smaller birds joined in the early morning chorus with all the neighborhood birds. An ordinary day in every respect.

Except that this was the day of the monthly neighborhood party, and this afternoon it was being held here. Lots to do. I hauled out folding chairs from the downstairs closet, shook out well-used cloth tablecloths and napkins, and started thinking of food: usually we had a buffet, everything from a platter of cold meats to carrot and celery sticks and radish flowers complete with onion dip, some sort of fruit bowl, and, of course, a nonalcoholic punch. As I said, lots to do.

The block party was a success, everyone said so, except for a small moment when I was introduced to someone's mother, a crone who looked to me for all the world like a Grimm's Fairy Tales wicked witch, a nasty woman who kept shaking a finger in my face and muttering something about my house not wanting me and downfalls to come.

The old woman was hurried away by her embarrassed daughter and I was left with a shaky feeling which I soon shook off. I had a house to clean up.

It wasn't until late that night that I noticed something amiss. At first, all I felt was a sort of itching in between my shoulder blades. You know, that feeling you get when you sense someone watching you, or of something going to go horribly wrong at any second.

And I thought I heard something sort of scrabbling in the wall beside my French doors which lead out onto the paved area before greenery starts. Then I could swear I heard a rustling, like a wind that can't make up its mind as to which direction it wants to blow in, a rustling like that, over there, in the corner of the yard, all the way down to the end of my piece of land where it ends in a narrow alleyway running horizontally alongside. Somewhere there in a corner, some thing was setting up a noise. A shimmery racket, building in volume. Shaking all the leaves on all the plants. To get my attention? To get my goat? To get at me?

I didn't know and wasn't about to go and investigate. In films, silly people are always going to see what's making a strange, an unusual, noise and end up with their heads chopped off, or some such.

I chose instead to ignore what was going on down there and focused my attention on the scrabbling noise in the wall. That was most likely a mouse, several mice, a rat, a trapped creature. And that was fixable.

The next morning I looked in my phone book—a positive luddite throwback, me, I resort to books in any form whenever possible in this age of information whizzing around the planet unseen—and found an exterminator. I rang and spoke with the person who answered in a nice, cheery voice saying,

"Hello There! Vermine Begone at Your Service! How May We Be Of Help!" I heard the capital letters and exclamation marks coming down the phone wire at me. And liked it. It gave me confidence; that the Vermine Begone person was so cheerful and positive rang a good note with me.

We set it up. A Vermine Begone exterminator would come over on Thursday? Thursday, I agreed, feeling very safe all of a sudden.

Vermine Begone would take care of the scrabbling noise and then this itchy sense I still had would vanish and my days could proceed as usual from starting well to ending likewise.

Was that my downfall? Trusting in an exterminator to rid me of unwanted influences that day, or any day? Because the next day, two days before Thursday announced itself, my ex phoned to demand money. I told him to go screw himself to the wall and he got positively nasty. Since I don't like hearing words like that, I hung up on him. He rang back. Continuously. All day. To the point where I had to disconnect the phone from the wall.

All was then well. My itchy feeling subsided, the scrabbling noise had ditto, and all of the leaves on all of the bushes at the end of my garden were quiet.

Then it all turned to crappola again. The scrabbling noise came on again, this time louder and running up and down inside the wall, the rhody bushes positively thrummed as if in agitation of a pending doom, the ex showed up on my doorstep with an angry red face and shaken fist threats, my beloved best friend told me she was moving to Angola and wished me luck with it all, and finally my washing machine threw a hissy fit and flung soapy water all over my kitchen.

Finally, Thursday. As promised, a representative of Vermine Begone showed up, did all sorts of listening and wall thumping tests, and pronounced the wall clear of anything. Nothing living in there at all, ma'am.

But what, I wailed, is making that noise?

What noise, Vermine Begone asked? Silence. The wall was giving up nothing as Vermine Begone and I stood in front of it, waiting for some kind of something. No thing occurred and Vermine Begone left.

You know as well as I do that it started up as soon as the exterminator had left my premises. And it was inevitable that the whole of my back garden started in a-rattling and a-rolling, sending up such a racket that the neighbors started phoning with complaints that my garden was keeping their animals, their children, their elders, awake all through the nights, worrying their sanity during the days.

After a month of neighborly harassment, I decided to torch the place. Wasn't that attached to it, never really liked it all that much, if truth be told. Send the curse into flames forevermore. Collect on the insurance, go somewhere else, start over. All of which I did with the help of a rather disreputable person who shall remain ever nameless, a ruffian of the first order who knew all about how to set untraceable fires.

I'm writing this from my hammock at the edge of the sea on on a white sandy beach in Rio. My little house, more a shack really, has remained silent ever since I arrived over a month ago. I can feel myself finally starting to relax.

But then, wait, I hear a scrabbling in one of the shanty walls. Could it be? Has it followed me? Am I going insane? Listen. It's there. No, over there. Hear it? Well? Is it a mouse? Mice? A rat? Don't tell me it's nothing! No thing at all! Why are all the palm trees waving frantically, the cacti shaking their spines?

Here comes that itchy feeling between my shoulder blades again!!

End of the Line

Matilda stretched and let slip a satisfied sigh. She sat up, turned around three times, and scrunched down again on the ragged truck seat. She was big enough to lay her head against the open window ledge and stay on the truck seat, although some of her hind quarters sloped off the seat's edge. Matilda didn't mind; her third favorite thing in her doggy life was, after eating and sleeping, driving around with Wilbur in his 1958 Slant 6 Dodge short bed pickup truck.

Matilda and Wilbur'd been hanging out together for a long time, as long as Matilda could remember. Sometimes he wasn't that good a companion, like when he forgot to feed her, or let her out in the mornings, or when he sometimes returned after a long time being somewhere else.

This morning, he let Matilda out late, didn't feed her, and bustled her into the pickup. Matilda didn't let his casual care of her bother her; she was in the truck and it was moving.

All too soon, the truck came to a screeching halt. Wilbur leaned over Matilda and opened her door. He pushed her old, quavering haunches. Pushed hard. Matilda, startled, at first pushed back but had to give up as she was too old to wrestle with Wilbur. She relaxed and was soon flying through the air.

She didn't feel anything except wind through her long hair coat until she landed. Hard. On something unforgiving. She had a split second of awareness, and then all of her, every piece of her, blacked out.

Until.

Matilda opened her eyes. All about her, above and below her, was white. A never-ending white. Matilda whined, frightened of all this nothingness. She kept whining, hoping her sound would shift this white, open it up, make it do something, and then saw shapes forming inside the white. The shapes took on edges, as if creating themselves anew.

Matilda saw puppies and kittens and horses and hampsters and guinea pigs and gold fish and birds of all sorts and old cats and dogs older than herself, all coming toward her. She opened her mouth to yowl and instead, out came,

"Where is this place?"

One of the older cats moved closer to her, a cat so old much of its hair had come off in clumps, leaving spots of ancient skin. This cat, followed as it was by the rest of the animals, seemed to be in charge, Matilda thought. She also wanted an answer to her question, so she asked it again:

"What is this place?" and noticed she wasn't, now, scared at all. So she put that thought into words—in this moment, she liked how the words felt inside her mouth.

"And why aren't I afraid of it?"

"This is an inbetween place," the elder cat said. "A place where you can rest, regroup, and reconsider."

Matilda felt more than observed all the animals forming a circle around her. Rather than feeling cornered, as she often did with Wilbur, she felt her whole inner body relaxing, as if time were rewinding and she was dissolving into her younger self inside her old outer body. And yet here she was. In this white, using words, talking to a very old, yet very young, cat. She asked her next question:

"Reconsider what?"

"What you want to do about it," said a three-legged mouse with a broken tail sitting on one of Matilda's shaggy feet.

All of the animals nodded. Yes. This is time to consider what you want to do about it.

The elder cat swiped at a section of the white and

pointed down through it. Matilda swivelled her head and looked. What she saw amazed her and yet it seemed completely right and natural to her that she should be able to look through this white thing and see the road she and Wilbur used to drive along, the country road where sometimes he'd let her out for a sniff round and, when she was younger, a run around. That road. In the early morning sunshine. And there, in the distance, was Wilbur's pickup, tooling along in an ambling fashion. She could watch it approach her sightline and hear him singing.

"Do it good to me now baby/do it to me slow." Wilbur laughed and grabbed at his crotch, singing the line again. He was on his way home from a long night with Zelda, she of the magnificent everything, hadn't yet showered, was still slightly drunk, and happy as ever Wilbur found happiness. He let go of his crotch and snatched up another beer from the stack on the passenger's seat. He popped open the top with his teeth and gave out a "Whooo!" The sun was up, he'd worn himself out; life was good.

Wilbur took another swig of his beer and started to launch into another set of dirty lyrics.

"There once was a man from Nantucket..."

Matilda, watching from the elevated white, turned to the elder cat and said,

"I consider that this should be the end of Wilbur."

"Not a problem. All you have to do is do to him what he did to you."

Matilda thought about that for a quick moment. Then she extended one paw through the opening.

Suddenly, because it happened just that way, all of a sudden, Wilbur noticed a cloud covering the sun over his pickup. He shook his head to clear his vision, stuck it out the window, and stared at the overhead cloud. None in front of him; he checked the rearview, none behind. Just overhead. Wilbur pulled his head in and shook it again. Nothing for him to worry about, just some weird weather thing going on.

The cloud came closer as Matilda moved her paw ever nearer to Wilbur's moving pickup truck.

Wilbur had one quick exclamation of, "What the fu...???" before Matilda's cloud paw crushed Wilbur and his truck into roadkill.

"End of the line, Wilbur," she said.

The animals all cheered.

Feckless Thugs

Widowed Mabel Cronk isn't dead yet. Just worn out. Not from any terminal disease. Not as a result of prolonged trauma or being run over by a truck.

From her feet.

Mabel Cronk's feet have been giving her gyp ever since they first hit the floor, pavement, hard pack, cement, turf, moss, forest floor, sand, beach, hard pack. With cramp, sting, burn, twitch, ache, throb, stab, pang, pain, twinge, sore, cold, wet, chafe.

She feels afflicted, distressed, algetic, dolorous, hurtful, in agony misery racking torment torture, and ultimately betrayed by her feet.

Tiny Genevieve Truefoil stares at her pea green carpet. Of all the pieces and parts of her rented one room apartment at the top of the 1920's shingled converted house she hates most, it is that pea green carpet. For some reason, the damn thing picks up, or possibly gives birth to, small, tight, rolls of white paper. Tiny things, less than the length of one of her fingernails—all ten nails always left long and filed to rounded points—the rolls seemed to hatch on their pea green field. One day, none appeared. The next, two, no three; then three and seven. If she doesn't pick them or vaccuum them up, she has a feeling these have the power to overwhelm her tender mind and send her into wishing for suicide.

Of deeper concern to Genevieve is her new neighbor, a rotund woman who wears pink curlers day in day out with no covering, a shouting woman who claims to have been an abductee. By aliens. In a mothership. Who claims that this apartment building/converted house is the next target. For what, Genevieve one day wondered out loud. For abductions, what else? Genevieve's wishes for suicide grow daily along with shouting woman's dire predictions.

Retired university professor Paula Klatmeiker is having escalating trouble relating to customer service people down the phone lines and in shops.

Her responses when some clerk asks, "Are you sure you've never been in our (fill in the blank) before," after she's already said she's never been there before, are sounding like this:

"No, I've never been here before; I made it up because I like to tell lies.

Yes, I was here before but you may not remember me as I was a gnome then and my voice was much higher and gravelly.

No, I've never been here before, but then you can't trust anything I say because I've spent the last twenty five years in an asylum for the insane. My insanity came about when people refused to listen to me.

Yes, I was here before, but I've forgotten everything that happened before…what?

No, I've never been here before and if you do not stop asking me that question, if you refuse to listen to me, all of your insides will start turning to mush and leak out your orifices. If you don't believe me, what's that sloshing sound coming down the phone line?"

Paula Klatmeiker is royally pissed off. At just about everyone.

Today Mabel decides to take her self and her miserable feet out. Of life. She walks into her neighborhood pawn shop and announces to the attendant, "I. Am. In. Need. Of. A. Gun." (Mabel frequently speaks in single word sentences, especially when in the presence of strangers or when she isn't telling the whole truth, as in this instance. That sentence should be, I am in need of a gun because I am taking myself and my miserable feet out.)

Today Paula looks a possible remedy to all this nonsensical nonlistening squarely in the face and so ends up at the pawn shop. "I. Am. In. Need. Of. A. Gun."

The clerk, a young man who took the job just for something to do between university terms, thinks he'd better get his boss, and fast. There's some weird shit going down here, he thinks. Needs a boss to sort it.

But there's never one around when the clerk needs one, so he's on his own. What to do? Sell them the guns? Be haunted ever more by the notion of these two old ladies taking themselves out in front of him (for the clerk these women, hardly pushing sixty who consider themselves yet sprightly, are knocking on the door to the temple of death. Which, actually, they are, but he doesn't think that way. He thinks that they won't do it, won't shoot the things at each other, won't have a bloody shoot-out in his store, well, his while he's behind the counter part-time.

Fuck it.

He's not getting paid enough for this so he bails, leaving the women staring at his backside as he vamooses out the door.

"It's my feet," says Mabel to the dust he leaves behind.

"No one listens to me anymore," says Paula to the space in between.

The women, strangers until this split second moment, this irrevocable decision-turning-on-a-sentence moment, look at each other. Each knows that an unspoken contest is beginning, a rivalry, a final encounter, a reckoning.

Who will rid themself of their affliction first? How will we know who wins? One of us will be dead and so there'll be no one to gloat with? That's no fun. Let's make up some rules and we have to decide how we're going to do this, anyway.

Then Genevieve Truefoil arrives on the scene. Ready to commit pea green carpeticide, or suicide, whichever comes first. "I. Am. In. Need. Of. A. Gun."

Then it becomes clear. With three of them, the potential exists for a witness, a remainder, a someone left behind to tell the tale, clean the sweep, erase the hurt.

For hurt it is.

Mabel's feet. Paula's invisibility. Genevieve's paranoia.

While the three were silently, to themselves, figuring out who should be shot first, the shop door slammed open. All of the wall-hung guitars and stacked up old VCR's, trombones and accordions and wooden chairs hanging from the ceiling and trunks and dented valises and many pairs of dirty galoshes and one glass case filled with flashy jewelry and the glass-topped counter holding weaponry of all sorts, the whole interior of the shop trembled at the thunderous approach of a large, bulky, determined woman well past a certain age who stomped heavybooted up to the counter, slapped a beefy palm down on it, creating a slim-line crack in the glass, and shouted, "Shop!" When no one appeared, she brought her fist up in preparation for another onslaught against the fragile glass counter. Just before flesh met glass, Mabel piped up. "No one here."

The new arrival, one Myrtle Quoi, spun around and shouted in Mabel's face, "I. Am. In. Need. Of. A. Gun!"

Genevieve, sheltering herself behind Paula's slim flanks, offered a little voice, "So're we all."

Paula nodded. "For the deed," she said in loud, school teachery tones.

"Which deed?" Myrtle demanded.

Mabel, having gathered herself and her long ago, pre-marriage confidence up around her like a woven shawl, said, rather proudly, "To take ourselves out."

Myrtle considered the other three for a moment:

she saw women like herself, of that age when nothing ventured nothing gained becomes a daily meditation because, at the end of the day, who the hell cares anymore? They are scrap heap material, and here they are, deciding to do something about it.

"How're you gonna do it?" she asked them, a cheer inherent in her tone.

"We were just working that out when you arrived," Paula said.

"We thought maybe two to shoot each other, the third to tell our stories and then shoot herself. Later." said Genevieve.

Myrtle liked the look of these ladies but knew they clearly hadn't had time to think the thing through. Their way sounded much too messy and could involve cops and lawyers. And the one group of people on the planet Myrtle couldn't abide was lawyers. How many lawyers does it take to screw in a lightbulb? As far as Myrtle is concerned, the bulb should short out and fry them all.

"So what's your beef? With the world? What's it for?" Myrtle asked all three.

"For my feet." "For my invisibility." "For my paranoia."

Mabel ventured to ask Myrtle the same question. "What's your beef, then?"

"I don't like cell phones and I don't like young people texting when they're sitting smack dab next to each other and I don't like the planet dying under a heavy blanket of plastic cast offs and I don't like politicians who're only in it for the bucks and I don't like the rich getting richer off the backs of the poor and I don't like doctors telling me that their medicines are any better than my own common sense and I especially don't like people telling me who I am or should be. So I want out. My beef is I don't belong in the world as it is now." She took a breath and a long look round the shop.

Something caught her eyes. "But I have a better idea."

Myrtle walked over to the shop window. She reached in and removed a sign which she held up. "Didn't you three notice this when you came in?"

All three wagged their heads in the negative. "No, of course we didn't," said Paula. "Too busy trying to buy our guns," said Genevieve. "Too self-focused," remarked Mabel.

Myrtle pointed at the sign: "See, this shop's for sale."

"So?"

"So, instead of shooting each other here and now and everything getting all messy and even worse, we buy the place. That way we keep an eye on the weapons and each other. What do you say?"

Genevieve, Paula, and Mabel swiveled their heads to look at each other and back at Myrtle. Some kind of secret signal passed between them, odd on such slight acquaintance, but there nevertheless. Myrtle picked up on it and laughed.

"Why don't we get acquainted first? I'm Myrtle. Myrtle Quoi." She held out her hand which was shaken by Paula, Mabel and Genevieve in turn. "Paula Klatmeiker," "Mabel Cronk," "Genevieve Truefoil."

It was, eventually, after the women retired to a nearby bar for ales and burgers that Myrtle offered to put up a fourth of the money if the other women would come in with her. It would be, she said, a grand last adventure before the cancer ate up her innards. Paula pointed out that the shop sale included a large, three-bedroom apartment upstairs, that the whole building was for sale (she'd read the small print at the bottom of the For Sale sign). Genevieve said she'd be willing to pitch in and would do any redecorating that needed doing. Mabel took some convincing, but finally agreed on the plan, if she could name the place. She'd heard a phrase on television once she liked—Feckless Thugs.

So it was decided. The four would buy the building, live upstairs, run the shop, and keep eyes on each other.

The only sore spot was Myrtle's cancer which, she said, could take her out anytime. They all agreed to write up an agreement about how to divide the property should Myrtle pop off soon.

The day she did that was three years down the road. In the between time, Feckless Thugs did a raring business. Partially because people in the town came to know that the women always gave fair prices for pawn, and also because tourists just loved hearing the story of how the shop came to be.

They never did shoot each other, but there were two lawyers, one former husband, and several customer service people who went strangely missing. Mabel's feet cleared up, Genevieve was never plagued by tiny paper rolls or alien neighbors again, Paula took a delicious vow of silence, and Myrtle, well, before she died, Myrtle kept on roaring her way through life.

In her newspaper eulogy, a reporter dubbed Myrtle Queen of the Feckless Thugs. The other three agreed it suited her and saluted her with a very expensive bottle of wine and fired a twenty-one gun salute (each firing seven rounds) over the roof of the Feckless Thugs Pawn Shop.

In The Beginning

It was only in the beginning of filming out on California's Mojave desert that Harley sensed a disturbance. First it seemed to generate itself from within the grips; then it spread to the lighting crew, then to camera, swooping through the actors, and landing on the director. Once they got through the second day, all seemed back on track. Until the horses refused to trot in the wide angle escape scene. All seven of them put their heads down to crop grass and refused to budge. When their handlers came up to them, they bolted to a new patch of fodder.

Then Harley was certain he was firmly jinked; this picture was going to end up on the cutting room floor like all his other attempts. He'd get a project into development, start filming, and blam. Disaster would strike and Harley would end up getting so stoned he wouldn't be able to get out of bed even if Hitch himself had risen from the dead and offered him a million dollar picture deal.

Harley was in trouble. Worse, he knew it. He couldn't fake his way out of this one.

On Saturday the sky opened up and sent rain down. Sheets of the stuff. Everyone's tempers were so frayed Harley told them all to take the day off, even the horses; especially the horses.

Harley's day off found him staring into an antique store window in Santa Monica as if his life depended on him seeing something in there. "Well," he thought, "my life couldn't get much worse so why not."

Harley walked into the crowded, dark little shop, almost walked into a Victorian breakfront, very nearly tripped over a collection of bone china chamber pots, definitely careened into an ancient three-wheeled bicycle, and ended up standing upright in front of a long wooden counter that had a glass and marble top. Edged in gold. Harley wondered if the gold were real and was just about to scratch at it with a fingernail when a voice inquired,

"You gonna buy sompin or jes' hulk aroun'?"

Harley pivoted; the voice revealed itself as belonging to a tiny, weasel-faced woman whose face seemed covered in hair clumps. Harley gulped. "Just looking," he said. And repeated himself.

"Better you buy somethin'," weasel face said. "Like this." She rummaged behind the counter and held up a bronzed oil lamp affair, dusty and grimy with the grunge of the ages. "You be wantin' this. Forty bucks. No returns."

Weasel face held out the object with one hand, her other palm up waiting for it to be crossed with silver. Harley, never one to assert himself in anything in his life, dug in his wallet, pulled out two twenties, put them in the open palm, grabbed up the object, and trotted in the general direction of the street, stepping on a stack of framed prints on his way out the door.

At home, Harley considered the thing, considered he'd like it to be cleaned, and set about doing just that. He found some brass cleaner at the back of his under-the-sink space in the kitchen and an old rag, and had just worked up a good rubbing rhythm when suddenly his kitchen was filled with smoke. Just as suddenly, the shape of a figure appeared inside the smoke and a voice said,

"Three wishes."

Harley dropped the lamp and shivered in his shoes. This couldn't be happening, not to him, no one ever offered him anything. He rubbed his eyes, but couldn't get rid of the smoke cloud or the wavering figure.

"Okay, okay," he said in the general direction of the voice. "My first wish is..." Here Harley had to think, but only for a moment—what would it be like to be back before all his woes began, how might his life change?

"To be fourteen again."

"Granted," said the voice.

And Harley stood there in his fourteen year-old body, wondering what the hell. A part of him, the grown up part, knew he couldn't do anything, had no money or skills, no power as a fourteen year-old boy. So he asked, "Second wish?"

The voice said, "What is your second wish?"

"To be my regular age again."

And so he immediately became the Harley of now. Harley the loser, Harley the lost.

"Can I have one more wish?" he asked the smoke.

"What is your last wish?"

Harley didn't hesitate at all. "To go back to the beginning, and in the beginning of my life, make it come out right."

Harley's body vanished. He'd gone back to his beginning, a thought, a midnight tussle, a sweaty coupling, a bunch of cells.

The figure melted in the smoke, the smoke dissipated, the weasel-faced woman left the shop; she and it vanished as if swallowed up into some other universe.

Would Harley come back in some other form? The answer would only come in the beginning of his new life, if there is such a thing.

Into the Night

Imagine two people sitting at a wooden park table with attached benches, facing each other from their opposite sides. Suppose it is twilight; the view in front of them is a countryside landscape, an Elysium sort of place. Perhaps a slow-moving river, some water birds, a few bats catching their dinners. Maybe even some cumulous clouds bearing tomorrow's rain, holding this evening's scattered daylight as it drops into night.

"Into the night of the dark black light," says one.

"No. It's, 'Into the light of the dark black night,' George Harrison," says the other.

"I like to think of night as having a dark black light," says one.

"I suppose night is all dark black light," says the other.

"What if it isn't?"

"What do you mean?"

"What if it's like Alice's looking glass?"

"You're losing me," says the other.

"Think on it like this. Suppose you, like Alice, step into the night and find yourself on the other side. In the dark black light."

"Are there strange creatures there, like hookah smoking caterpillars?"

"Wrong book—that's Alice's Adventures in Wonderland. Clearly you don't know your Alice."

"I know my Beatles, especially Geo. Harrison."

"Well, not knowing your Alice is like your guitar gently weeping," says one. "And I want to step into the night. Before dinner."

"You're losing it."

"No. Just hungry. I think. Or maybe I'm yearning. For something. Unnameable."

"Maybe what's what insanity is, stepping into the

night. Sort of," says the other.

"I think it's more than that," says one.

"Say more."

"Suppose it's like stepping into a changing place."

"A changing place."

"Hmmm. And from there, well, I don't know what happens from there because I haven't managed it yet."

"Haven't managed what?"

"Going into the night. Haven't you been listening?" says one. "I saw this TV program about radio astronomers in Australia. Building sci-fi looking telescopes over acres of land in the red desert land. They call it ASKAP, Australian Square Kilometer Array Parameter, or something like that. And with these telescopes they're trying to find out what our place is in the universe."

One pauses.

"So, what if our place is somewhere into the night? What about that? Someplace inside one of those wonderful cosmic images, those colorful nebula sent to the Hubble telescope, like those. Suppose our place is there, and all we have to do is step into the night?"

Silence for a beat, then the other says,

"All I can say, is, wear your walking shoes."

Imagine that in the building on the slope behind the two lights come on in a few windows. The other stands up. "Coming in to dinner?"

One's head shakes, no. The other walks away.

One sits a long time, eyes closed, watching without seeing the sun announce its departure from the sky with an orange and gold burst then slope away and let the night take it.

Suppose a day a week later when a small notice appears in the local newspaper.

"Muriel Dawson, an amateur astronomer in her day, was found sitting on a bench outside the senior residence where she'd been living for the past 10 years.

The smile on her face gave passers-by the impression she was still living so no one bothered her for days."

It was the other who had realized and pocketed the note in her hand which said, merely, "I've managed it. Goodbye."

Suppose. Imagine.

It's a Myth

"'It was the myth of fingerprints.'"

"What was?"

"Oh, nothing. A line from a Paul Simon song."

"My favorite is 'hints and allegations...accidents and incidents'...something like that."

"'I can call you Betty, Betty when you call me You can call me Al.'"

"Why are we talking about Paul Simon songs?"

"Because we don't want to talk about IT."

"'You're shaking my confidence daily.'"

"Different album."

"I know. So. What are we going to DO about IT?"

"Why do we have to do anything about it?"

"We have to do something about IT, we can't keep on having this argument about it and we do have to do something about it because IT sucks us dry."

"Oh, now, you're being a bit harsh, don't you think?"

"No, I don't. It's a myth, the whole thing. It's monsters under the bed and in our minds. IT takes us away from who are are. IT isn't real."

"Still, I don't see why...?"

"Because I want IT gone. Is that enough reason for you?"

"Wow. Are you sure? I mean, once it's gone, we won't..."

"I'm well aware of what we won't. I want IT gone. And I think you do, too, really."

"Well, okay. Whatever you want, Al."

"I'm Al, you're Betty."

"Whatever. But are you sure you're sure? It'll be over in a month or a year at best, a short-time phenomenon that lives out its short life and then IT won't bother us anymore."

"Do you really believe that?"

"I do."

"Well, I don't. I think IT is evil. The opposite of good. Of thinking. Of reason. Of curiosity. Name your best ever 'shot at redemption' and IT is anti that."

"Okay, okay, okay, okay, okay! Out IT goes then!"

"I love you, Betty."

"And I you, Al. Or am I Betty?"

IT got placed carefully on the curb in front of Betty and Al's apartment building the next day, a soft summer's day as it happens. They put a sign on IT, Please Take Me, but no one did, that day or the next, or the days after.

Summer turned to Fall, shed leaves fell upon IT, dogs lifted their legs against IT, a few careless folk smudged their cigarettes out on IT. Circling birds shat upon IT. Garbage from the garbage trucks drifted onto IT. Someone shot at its back cardboard panel with a pellet gun. The cycling newspaper boys stuck old gum to IT. Frequently.

Rain fell on IT, along with some mighty hail which pocked it. Snow came and covered IT along with all the cars parked on that side of the street. When the snow melted, there IT stood, damaged to within an inch of its life.

It was at this moment that Corey Smith happened by and spotted IT. IT called to him; he later told a friend it had felt like a Siren call. He had to have IT. But what, asked the friend once he'd looked at IT, are you going to do with this thing?

Corey, being a budding anti-establishment artist and definitely a child of his century, instantly set IT up against a white wall without changing an iota of its size or shape or general ruination and photographed IT with his iPhone. He then posted the photo on Facebook with the quip, "What do you think this is?"

Corey had one response to his post: "I think I want it, where are you?" signed, Fharl Tombey, Dayton Ohio Twentieth Century Cultural Art Museum.

Intrigued, Corey met with Fharl. Fharl took one look at it in person, gave Corey $250,000 for his piece of Twentieth Century Cultural Art, and promptly had IT installed in the permanent exhibit hall at her museum.

Corey, meanwhile, trotted off to find some more discarded sidewalk treasures he could turn into hard cash.

Fharl, being very clever when it came to art work placement, arranged IT a few feet away from a startlingly white wall, resting on an equally startlingly white section of floor, raised IT up a bit on a wooden block painted a startling white so that it looked like it was floating above an invisible throne, and had white velvet stanchion ropes and posts put around IT. She wanted patrons to look, think; not touch.

She arranged a series of three spot lights: one shone towards the back of IT; the original back cardboard shot-wrecked panel of the cabinet had been removed so all of ITS innards were visible. One shone in a circle spot in front of IT, indicating where a patron would, even should, be drawn to stand. And the last shone directly onto the glass of the cathode ray tube. This last light created an effect of a golden eye staring back at the viewer.

Fharl mounted a perfectly sized, beautifully hand-lettered sign—stark black inked letters placed against a stark white background—to dangle in perpetuity from the velvet rope. It read,

"It's a Myth?"

Making a Pizza

Patience Pendergast pondered the array of ingredients, chopping board, and crockery bowl arranged before her on the wooden kitchen table. In one hand, she held her favorite chopping knife, an 8-inch Four Star Henckels Cooks Knife. In the other hand, she held a yellow faded and deeply-creased-from-many-foldings piece of paper. She turned her attention to this ancient missive and read aloud:

"Prunella Pendergast's Perfect Pizza Pie Preparation. Begin your preparation by gathering all of your thirteen P ingredients."

Patience counted out: "Pepperoni, pineapple, persimmon, paprika, peppers (red, green, chilli), proscuitto, pansies, papaya, parrot fish, Portobello mushrooms, pecorino, parmesan, partridge."

She carried on reading aloud as if lecturing a group of kitchen wannabes. "Cut all into chunks, toss in a bowl, and spread onto a pre-prepared crust, saving the cheeses for last. Shred these all over the rest, throw the completed Pizza in a very hot oven, take out when done, serve and eat. For those diners with weak stomachs, gag and throw up. And then, don't invite those people over for Pizza ever again. Much too messy."

Patience folded up the paper, tucked it into a hip pocket, picked up her Henckels and started chopping. She began with the partridge and the parrot fish because Prunella left no instructions about plucking or cleaning a bird nor for deboning a fish, so Patience had to rather hack at these items before feeling satisfied they were in chunk size, whatever that was, and she actually had no idea and wasn't admitting that small fact to herself.

Once these were chunked and tossed in the bowl, Patience started in on the meats. Then she'd move to the vegetables, fruit, and flowers and the cheeses.

This was her usual order of events. Today, however, Patience grew bored halfway through chunking up the parrot fish. And boredom was Patience's bête noir; Patience the Impatient, Prunella had dubbed her back in Patience's pretty little girl days. This day boredom caused Patience to lose her focus, shift her chopping hand slightly, and allowed her beloved Henckels to chop off the end of her pinky finger.

Patience, her brain not yet receiving the pain signal, kept chopping. Then two things occurred at once: Patience felt the stabbing sting, and looked down to see her finger, or seven-eighths of it, throbbing and pulsing out blood, spurting it judiciously about the chopped up parrot fish.

Patience stared at this anomaly to her grandmother's receipe for the Perfect Pizza Pie Preparation for a beat. Then she turned, picked up a kitchen towel, wrapped that around her finger and returned to stare down at the tip her finger, complete with nail, staring back up at her.

Without a moment's hesitation, she scooped it up, tossed it in the bowl with the two fishes pieces, and carried on chopping and slicing. This, she thought, made for a change and was anything but boring.

Halfway through her ministrations, when she was about to shred the cheeses, she removed the towel, squeezed the base of her finger, and dropped blood into the bowl. She stirred everything up. She gave an extra run through all the bowled ingredients with her knife to make sure the finger end, complete with its nail, was fully combined into her Perfect Pizza Pie Preparation.

Cheeses loaded on, oven hot, she slid the thing in to bake, sat down, and, taking a pen from a shirt pocket, added a few words to Prunella Pendergast's admonitions:

"If you happen to slice off any of your own body parts and want to add them in, make sure they are fully incorporated before baking. Enjoy."

Passing By

"So what do we do now?"

"We wait."

"For how long?"

"Stop bouncing around, Oversoul 28. People on Earth are going to think this cloud is full of lightning even though the sun is shining and then they won't know what to do with themselves. Your job is not to call attention to your self."

Still bouncing, casting its light beam here and there, the younger Oversoul 28 couldn't help a snide rebuttal: "But I don't have a self. You told me that, Oversoul 22. My first day in training."

Oversoul 22 heaved a huge sigh, or rather its light spark quivered violently for an earthly second. As if to itself, it said, "Oh, the impatience of youth."

"I heard that, you know," Oversoul 28 said, but with respect and a smile, if it could smile.

Of course, Oversouls don't talk in human terms. Rather, their thoughts bounce across time and space, connecting up in strands of consciousness and understanding all through all the universes. These two Oversouls, one student, one teacher, dedicated to watching over earthlings, were at present hovering on the edge of a generously fashioned cumulonimbus cloud, waiting.

"If you'll behave yourself and make your light beam lighter, smaller, more discrete, I'll tell you what we're doing here," said Oversoul 22.

Oversoul 28 obediently dimmed to unrecognizable size.

"We're waiting for Flight UAL457 out of LAX headed towards O'Hare," 22 said in its best teacher voice. "Once that flight is directly passing by this cloud, at that instant in Earth time, our task is to..."

"Let me say this part," interrupted 28 with full

youthful vigor. "We stop it and enter the cabin and find three people who are going to survive the crash." 28 paused. "But I don't understand how the people aren't going to know their plane has stopped in mid air, and I don't understand what happens when..."

22 stepped in. "You don't need to understand, 28, but I'll explain how this works. Because you do need to have an inkling of what's coming." Oversoul 22 disappeared for a moment, then reappeared.

"Just checking. The flight will be here very soon, so listen carefully," it said.

"Flight UAL457 will pass directly by our cloud and we will stop it with our combined energy. All the passengers and crew will feel, will know, is a small bump, like hitting a bit of turbulence. Once we direct ourselves inside, we will search each soul to find the ones we have been instructed to find."

28 couldn't help itself: "But how will we know who they are? And who's instructing us, anyhow? I thought you were in charge?"

Again, 22 quivered, this time making itself grow huge and tiny in less than a millimeter of a nanosecond of Earth's time. "I've told you again and again. I'm your Oversoul for this sector. When you've completed your training, completed this last assignment, you'll become an Oversoul of your own sector. All of the Oversouls are in charge of each other for everything. Okay now?" 22 doesn't wait for 28 to respond. "We will instantly sense who is going to survive. You will connect with one, and this one will be in your charge throughout their earthly lifetime. I will connect with the other two."

Of course 28 couldn't help itself: "But why do I only get one?"

22, with great patience, said, "You are young yet and we all start with one. Once you've proved that you can guide without interfering in your human being's life, you'll be offered more. But now, here comes our flight. Ready yourself, 28."

Inside the cabin of Flight UAL475 out of LAX, currently starting its climb over the Colorado Rocky Mountains, some of the passengers slept, some read, some watched the inflight movie, some played on iPads, some talked to their neighbors, some fussed with their young children, and three felt a slight hit of turbulence.

"Hope this doesn't continue," said the pilot to her co-pilot, George. At the same time she said that, she felt an odd pressure on her left arm, which she ignored as she focused her attention on the dials in front of her.

Sara-Lee, the First Class attendant, popped her head in to the flight deck and asked, "Honor, was that turbulence I felt a sign of things to come?"

"Nothing to worry about, Sara-Lee," said the pilot. "If any of the passengers are nervous, reassure them, will you?"

Sara-Lee nodded and withdrew. Returning to the passenger cabins, she felt a slight pressure on her right arm, which she promptly forgot about as one small person called her attention.

"Miss, oh miss, did you see that?" The small person was one Heather Lampdon, aged 12, travelling on her own to go stay with her grandmother in Chicago.

Sara-Lee bent down to talk to Heather. "What's that, kiddo?"

Heather swivelled her head and pointed out the window; her curtain was up and sun shone through like a beacon. "There, on that cloud. I saw a spark, two sparks like, like it was beeping at us. That cloud there."

Heather turned her head back; her eyes met Sara-Lee's. "Did you see it?"

Sara-Lee obediently looked out the window as the cloud moved away. "No, honey, I didn't. Now. Would you like some crayons and a coloring book?"

Heather Lampdon pulled her small self up in

her seat. "I'm twelve," she said with great authority. Sara-Lee smiled and walked down the aisle. Just then, Heather felt a small tug on her forehead. She put her hand up to the spot, but the feeling left almost as soon as it arrived.

United Airlines Flight 475 lost control of itself with the help of a faulty fuel line and a sudden redirection of upper atmosphere wind currents, and plunged to the ground on a map coordinate in between Rifle (Lat. 39.5355) and Parachute (Lat. 39.449891), on the Western Slope of the Rockies. Only three people survived: one passenger, one crew member, and the pilot.

As if drawn by an unseen current, these three joined up. At first, through survivor guilt. Then, as time passed, each felt they would not be whole without the other two. And so they met, each year, and exchanged stories of their lives.

At every one of these meetings, two pin spots of light could be seen, if one could see them, hovering somewhere above the meeting—on a ceiling where the wall meets it, or on a high tree limb, for instance.

At the first of these meetings, Oversoul 28 asked Oversoul 22 what it was supposed to do? And Oversoul 22 replied,

"Your task is to pass by occasionally, to gently nudge your earthling's thoughts into realities."

"But what if those thoughts are harmful ones, or silly ones, or just plain dumb?"

"Remember. We are never to interfere. We are passing by Oversouls. As they will be one day."

Both Oversoul lights shimmered and danced, then flickered on and off, as if, one might say, they were laughing.

Dedicated to Jane Roberts, herself an Oversoul

Residue

Elder Baggett got the idea from a couple of Mormons who knocked on his apartment door, 2c, one evening when the mosquitos were thicker than a molasses summer. Both men wore white short-sleeved shirts with black ties and slapped their arms and necks as they handed Elder Baggett Joseph Smith's prophecy.

"My name's Elder Johnson and this here's Elder Wilson and he...we, were wondering whether you'd ever heard of The Book of Mormon." It was the blond Mormon who spoke as the brown-haired one stared at Elder Baggett's thick gray hair that sprouted up off his head like a rooster's cock comb, sprang out his ears and his nostrils, mottled his chin, sneaked up his shirt front.

When Elder Baggett's mother had pushed him out of her womb thirty-five years ago, she'd taken one look at him and fainted dead away, never again to be revived. His father had shouted, "Where's my son?! You gave birth to a hair ball, woman!" before he ran backwards out of town.

Elder Baggett was not enamored by The Book of Mormon, but he was interested in the two young men whose necks and arms were developing red welts which grew as they scratched each mosquito bite.

"Did you say your names was 'Elder'?" he asked.

"I'm Elder Wilson and this here's Elder Johnson," said the staring, brown-haired one.

"And you say you got yourselfs a Mormon book, eh?" asked Elder Baggett, measuring the space between his height and that of the two men standing in his doorway. He reckoned two full heads difference, maybe two and a half. He measured in his head, quick, while the two Elders were exchanging a look of their own.

"Do you suppose he has hair like that all down his back," signalled the eyes of Elder Johnson.

"Wouldn't it be too yummy for words to go skating in all that stuff," twinkled the eyes of Elder Wilson.

The Elders Johnson and Wilson frequently had wordless communiqués with each other—it was a mode of communication they'd perfected over their years together, and they had always used it to their great advantage.

Just now, they felt in complete control of the situation, and were eager to get to the finish line. "Yes, sir," Wilson told Elder Baggett. "We have the Book of Mormon and want to share it with you." He couldn't help a small giggle from jumping out of his mouth. Elder Johnson held his mouth still in eager anticipation.

"Well, now," said Elder Baggett, "I'm not in any hurry for books, but I could sure use some company. Whyn't you boys come in and set a spell? Rest your doggies?" With that, Elder Baggett turned his back and sloped into the dark reaches of his apartment.

The two Elders looked at each other; this was not was they expected. But what was life if not one gorgeous crap shoot? The Elders shrugged their shoulders in twin-like agreement, and followed Elder Baggett into the gloom.

Now, at the very same moment, the very ditto selfsame instant, Francine Baggett was waking up in her house on the hill clear across town. So clear across town was this house, a squat affair, painted various shades of bilious green, with porticoes where porches should be and columns where beams should be, so much on the outskirts of the town that also housed Elder Baggett in his apartment, that postal workers, just because they sometimes got bored sorting things, frequently forgot to deliver Francine's mail. They told her, those erstwhile postal workers, that mail that far out of town, that much outskirting, was probably in another postal code and she should take her complaints to those offices.

This morning, Francine's main complaint was her head pounding. To add insult to injury, the inside of her mouth felt full and furry, like the inside of a hot gym sock. Her joints ached; her crotch was afire. It took a long moment for Francine to remember the events of the previous night that had brought on such an inglorious wakening. But it all too soon came rushing back, a tumble of images coursing through her memory as her eyes tried to unglue themselves and focus on something outer.

Last night Francine had indulged as never before—chocolate cake and strawberry ice cream and butterscotch eclairs and five-layer napoleons and custard tarts and a bottle of a scintillating 1978 French Merlot and bushels of grapes and a saucepan of tapioca pudding and, finally, at dawn, C&H's best white sugar straight from the cardboard box through her lips, down her gullet. And then the masturbating. With a fury unseen or heard of in modern times Francine worked herself until her finger joints ached and seven batteries in her mini-sized, hard plastic vibrator crapped out.

Francine pulled herself out of bed. One thing was on her mind, once it came clear, and that thing was full on revenge. She was going to get the person responsible for her slide into sugar hell and make him pay, pay, pay. Oh, yes, one Elder Baggett, by name. If it hadn't been for him walking out of their suspended marriage last week, after their argument about his propensities, she wouldn't be waking up like a woman embalmed. Francine knew this morning after was not her fault. She would lay the blame on Baggett, where it oh so rightly belonged.

Francine stomped to the bath and filled it half full with sea salts and scalding water. She glared at the water as it ran into the porcelain tub, seeing Elder's face in the salt foam. She growled at the image until it melted. Then she lowered herself into the sitz bath and let it have its way with her body.

An hour later, Francine, her skin red and alive, sweat pouring from every gaping pore on her body, gulped down three, full, 8-ounce glasses of purified ice water, belched soundly, grabbed up her tote bag with the embroidered motto, G-I-R-L Goddess In Real Life, and jumped into her 1934 Duzenberg Convertible. She put the Duzie's top down and sang all the way across town, a song of her own making up, somewhat to the tune of "Onward Christian Soldiers." The thick clouds of mosquitos Francine Baggett and her stalwart Duzenberg roared through dissipated as if swatted by a hand much larger than God's or Joseph Smith's.

Not even mosquitos landed on Francine when she was on a mission.

Back in Apartment 2c, the three Elders were having themselves a time. Now, as to what sort of time, well, that's debatable because all that was ever found in the residue at apartment 2c was a mound of mosquito droppings, one frayed brown shoelace, a torn book cover with the words, Boo of Mo remaining, a clump of grey hair dotted with blood, and a rubber dildo of impressive proportions. This surely was enough fodder to keep tongues wagging for centuries, all going off in different directions, becoming positions from which folks had a hard time backing down.

Reporters sitting on swivel stools at Emma's Elevator Ice Cream and Candy Shoppe weeks after the fact consumed large amounts of sugar and spice while arguing the point. Locals, more comfortable dangling by their tailbones on stools at the Lost Town Tavern, worried the more discrete points with a toothsome zeal, not unlike dogs worrying succulent lamb shanks, while taking in gallons of whatever was on tap.

But if Elder Baggett, the two Mormon Elders and Francine Baggett herself were around to tell their side of the story, attention might have shifted over to the mosquitos, where it rightly belonged.

Elder Baggett's idea, when he brought those two unsuspecting, horny Mormons into his parlor, was to find out, would mosquitos shit more if they had more to eat? He'd been experimenting with bits of meat, rotten iceberg lettuce leaves, dead mice, dead cat, dead dog, collecting mosquito droppings, and now he was ready for the big test—humans—and he had two elders here to help him. He'd been waiting for a sign and surely three elders in a room was it.

What is the scene when Francine arrives? What does she do with the mosquito swarm that is following her? Do the mosquitos shit more once they get a taste of two elders and an Elder and a ripe Francine? Does Elder throw mosquito shit on Francine and so she's saved from any more bites? Does she run away?

What happened is this. Francine gets her revenge on Elder Baggett because once she arrives, he's sitting on top of two stunned elders, one of whom has a gigantic dildo in his left hand. Baggett is swatting away at mosquitos that won't leave him alone, which turn him into a quivering mass of mosquito bite flesh which is worrisome because, unbeknownst to Elder Baggett, he's deadly allergic to mosquito bites in quantity. A few his body will tolerate; more than that and he'll start losing consciousness; more than that and his brain will start to frizzle; more than that and all his blood will start seeping out every place it can seep out of.

So Francine takes this all in, heaving gigantic sighs, sighs profound enough to cause her to start shaking, partly in anger because it seems Elder Baggett is dying and what kind of revenge is that, and partly out of shock. Francine doesn't bother making the distinction. She just sighs.

Just then one of the elder Mormons groans and stirs. Then the other one. They push Elder Baggett's by now rigor mortising body off their own, maneuver themselves into sitting positions, have a silent communication with each other, and then heave themselves up to stand in front of Francine.

The mosquitos, those already in apartment 2c and those Francine unwittingly brought in with her, are in a frenzy of blood lust, all that succulent flesh just waiting to be stabbed and drained.

Francine Baggett, unaffected by mosquitos or dead husbands or Mormons clutching dildoes and anything else they might have about their persons or in their inclinations, does the only sensible thing. She hightails it out of there.

The Mormons, leaving their cherished Joseph Smith text, are a bit less elegant in their departure. They stagger out of apartment 2c shouting for a hospital, an ambulance, a police presence, shouting anything except a prayer or two or three.

The mosquitos, replete, satiated, zoom off out the door behind everyone else. True to their nature, they go on the hunt for another door, another feast.

Until a mosquito-savvy Benedictine nun in her convent's garden in the next town over sees them coming, removes a spray can of organic weed killer from the tool shed, and blows them into oblivion.

Sam and Janet Evening

1972. Sam had arrived early, hoping to hook up with some ditzy blonde, skip any getting-to-know you chat, and boogie on out. He was only here, at the community centre, because Fred and Nate said he could score big time tonight. Lots of eager pussy at a local village dance. So far, after checking out the field, he couldn't see what the fuss was about. After all, he wasn't out for a quick lay. Was he? He wasn't sure; he just knew he was bored to distraction. He moved over to stand against the wall nearest the band; maybe some sweet honey would mistake him for a drummer (*Yeah, right*).

Even above the band's shattering thump, Sam heard a new crowd hungering to squeeze in, laughing and shoving, hurrying to get moving to the beat. The only person there standing still, pinioned to the wall, lazing to perfection, he cast his eyes around the hall and into the heaving mass of newcomers.

There was something, he witnessed, an anomaly (*was that the word he wanted?*) in the midst of the boisterous throng. Someone quieter. He watched as a shadow of a girl was whipped from the happy bunch disbursing to different groupings scattered here and there about the hall.

Janet Evening, once flung, escaped to the closest wall. She flattened herself to it. There, behind a row of folding metal chairs, seated large-ankled matrons, resting dancers, and a few reluctant teens, she found comfort in becoming invisible (*isn't it best to be not seen or heard?*). The band geared up into full throttle; Janet Evening held her ground.

Just as she shook herself into determination to unpeel herself from her wall of safety and leave, go back to her soft cat, warm fire, fuzzy slippers and a glass or three of Stella, her familiar solitary life, her welcoming life, Janet Evening spotted Sam spotting her.

This was something new.

For both Sam and Janet Evening.

Even through the distance between them, Sam could feel her slender body, dressed in gossamer fabric, some flowery pattern, tender slippers on her narrow feet, pressed against the far wall, standing as if plastered to the thing, as if she would collapse if the wall suddenly vanished. He could sense subtlety rolling off of her and was pulled to it. He started to slowly cross the floor towards Janet Evening.

Janet Evening saw a slouching, rangy character, looking as if he'd just stepped out of an imitation James Bond flick—dark of slicked-back hair, clothing, and superior, laid-back attitude; a real died-in-the-wool bad boy, wearing no socks under his leather loafers. Exactly the kind of man her mother told her to run from; she moved toward him, deer in headlights, moth to flame (*any cliché would do*).

She felt breathless, inescapably dragged into his danger.

He felt undone, inevitably hooked on innuendo.

They met in the middle of the dance floor while around, over and under them, the band belted out a mid-60's recording, Boots.

For long minutes, they held each other's eyes as the mob gyrated and pulsed around them. (*The last two people.*)

They spoke at once, with hushed voices so as to not shake the moment away.

"I saw you," Sam said.

"I saw you," Janet said.

"You looked so scared."

"You look so dangerous."

Sam laughed a bit. "And yet still you came out here, to the middle."

"Well," she tossed back, "Maybe it's all an act with

me." A beat. "Maybe I'm the dangerous one," she said with false bravado.

"So I should be scared?"

"No. Never. Not of me."

"Nor me," Sam said.

The band shifted speed and sound up a notch to an Ike and Tina number. Sam and Janet Evening reached out and touched each other's hands. They held on, marooned in the middle of the heaving mass of dancers.

"I like this," Sam said.

"Do you have a name?" Janet asked.

"I'm Sam."

"I'm Janet."

"Come here often?"

Now she was the one to laugh. "Never been here before."

"Me, neither," Sam said.

"So what are we doing here tonight?" Janet asked in a smallish voice, loud enough for Sam to hear if he bent his head close to her mouth. Which he did.

Then he risked it. "I haven't a fucking clue."

Fast forward forty five years to a cottage in England's Yorkshire Dales. Tea time. Proper china tea service on a silver tray on a mahogany coffee table, chintz covered easy chairs pulled up in front of a sturdy fire, two rescue cats and one saved dog all snoozing on their hearth rugs. Sam using an old-fashioned toasting fork to brown two tea cakes, one for each. Janet finishing off a sketch for tomorrow's painting session.

"Do you remember," she says, "The last thing you said to me that night?"

"I haven't a fucking clue," Sam says. They chuckle, buttering and jamming their toasted tea cakes.

"I also remember I felt that you needed rescuing."

"Nah," Janet says, "you needed rescuing."

"We saved each other..." Sam starts it.

"...by crossing that crowded room," Janet echoes. (*Enchanted.*)

The Black Clock

I was left by my parents at a very early age—mine, not theirs—but in their flight from parenthood they left behind them an antique clock. A very antique clock. An ugly, in my now adult opinion, black marble clock.

Wherever I move it, it seems to squat with a disapproving air, as if I am to blame for its unseemly state of being. I've moved it to the top of my fireplace mantle. Placed it one end of the mantle, then the other. Then in the direct center. I've placed it on top of a bookcase, on one of the bookcase shelves, on my dining table (more of a small wooden square on stilts with an accompanying stool) and on my desk. Where it resides today.

Today is my birthday and I am determined to cleanse myself of anything unsightly in my life—and that certainly includes one

'Extremely Rare, circa 1870, Black Marble Mantel 15" x 14" x 7" Timepiece By Archille Brocot, Paris, the black marble case with canted and leaded corners inlayed with puffery marble, the substantial French movement by Archille Brocot with five going barrels and visible front Brocot escapement, the signed two-piece white enamel dial with Breguet blued steel hands and original numbered pendulum'

according to the brochure that came with it.

So out go the bell-bottomed jeans, the teapot that leaks when it pours, the photographs of my ex, all of the moldy food in the fridge, the once-upon-a-time dog bed, the stacking raatan baskets growing mites, and the *Extremely Rare, circa 1870, Black marble Mantle 15" x 14" x 7" Timepiece by Archille Brocot, Paris*, etc.

I chucked unreusables where such items belong and trundled the rest off to the nearest Salvation Army store. They took the dog bed, the teapot and the jeans, and refused the black clock. Much too valuable, they said. Better keep it or auction it off.

So off to auction the black clock went. And came back. Unsold.

Listed on an online auction site. Sat there like a stone. Unsold.

Offered it to a local antique shop. Declined. Unsold.

And then my back went out and I had other things to think about than a stubborn black clock.

I took up the challenge to rid myself of the hideous black clock by taking photographs of it, posting those on lampposts, in shops, in newspapers, and on social media sites. Still nothing.

Then a hail storm took out two of my bedroom windows and half of my ancient tile roof. Fixing all that took time away from the black clock situation.

One summer afternoon I sat on the sidewalk outside my house with it on a folding wooden TV table. I put up an accompanying sign: Extremely Rare, circa 1870 (well, you know where I'm going with this) Black Marble Clock. No reasonable offer refused.

No offers were offered. Oh, people stopped and looked the thing over, but no one actually committed to taking the thing. By the end of the day, I'd reduced its price to FREE!!!.

Still no go.

My final attempt was to give it to friends as a gift. Down the years, that clock made the rounds of all my friends—give it to one single, it ends up as a wedding gift. Give it to a couple, it ends up as a birthday gift for another single. And so on, until, about a decade later, it made its way back to me.

It is now 18 years since my parents left me the clock and today they returned. Out of the blue. No warning. No explanations. No sorry we left you alone when you were little, no how've you been. Just a request for their clock.

Hallelujah! And sing Hosannah! The black clock, the bane of my previous 18-year existence, was leaving my house. I handed over the clock with no more than a "Here it is" (I mean, why pick at old sores? Why ask, why'd you leave me with this thing? What did I expect them to say? Besides, picking at old wounds only gives you more sore places), and bid them goodbye.

Oh, this called for a celebration.

I was deep in the middle of a very superior bottle of wine and a scrumptious meal of perfectly charred chateaubriand with a crispy romaine salad followed by a superlative chocolate mousse when the phone rang.

"Is this you?" the voice asked.

"Yes, it's me," I replied.

"Well," the voice said, "your parents' car just plowed into the back of a lumber truck and they're dead. But all is not lost. There was a black clock on the back seat, some kind of antique deal, and it survived. Thought you'd want to know."

The Cooling Curve of Napthalene

Two Months Ago
"I say we call ourselves Bitches in Heat."
"That's horrible. Gross."
"Yeah, I agree. Gross. Think again."

The three girls sat in Rachel's dad's shed wearing their thinking caps, drinking bootlegged, from Sonia's mom's liquor cabinet, vodka, and generally chilling out, until Mina came up with another one.

"Okay, then, how's about The Chubbettes?"
"That's even worse."

Mina grabbed the Vodka bottle from Rachel, spilt some on her XX-Large Grateful Dead T-Shirt complete with holes, and took a huge swig. She wiped the mouth with the back of her tattooed hand, passed the bottle to Sonia.

Sonia shook her head, no, and didn't take it. "Can't. I'm on this fabulous diet."

"Amazing. Never thought you'd stick to it."
"Absolutely."

"You don't get it, like, it works." Sonia stood up and stretched her hands to the roof. She revolved slowly in front of her friends.

"See?" she said with pride. "I've lost 10 pounds already." She sat down again. "So no booze until I get another 10 off."

"Okay. So you're on a diet. Again. Good for you. Now, about our name. How's about, something combining our instruments? A whatchamacallit-gram," Mina said.

"Anagram," said Rachel. "That's not bad. What'll it be? How do you put keyboard, cello, and French horn into one word?"

All three drank more vodka and sat with furrowed, thinking, brows.

"KFC," Sonia, always thinking about food, offered.

"Taken," said Mina. "What about FCK?"

"Hey," Sonia said. "FCK. I like it. Sort of in your face name."

"We'll never get any gigs where there're little kids with that name, though," said practical Rachel. "Let's just keep on thinking. We'll come up with the perfect name for our band soon. Just you wait."

One Month Ago
Sonia arrived at the shed early. She'd brought a bottle of lemon-flavored water which she used to repeatedly rinse out her mouth. Before Mina and Rachel showed up, Sonia had on fresh makeup and had rinsed the vomit from the front of her loose shift.

"Hey, girl," Rachel said in greeting when she got there.

"What about, Horny Harlots," Sonia said. "I've always liked that word, harlot."

"We're not calling ourselves stupid names," Rachel added, "Wow, you've really lost a bunch of weight!"

Mina arrived on the heel of that sentence, and piped up with her own observation: "Is there anything of you left under that tent you're wearing, Sonia?"

The girls all laughed and then got down to some serious drinking. At one point in the late, late afternoon Rachel decided they should call themselves some combination of their names—Sonia, Mina, Rachel, only alphabetically. Or by their colors—black, white, yellow.

This got the girls laughing hysterically as they shouted out names like So-Ra-Me, Chania, Sina, Lorias, Yewack, and the like. They rather liked Sina and chanted it out loud getting louder on each chant until Rachel reminded them that her dad would be home soon and they didn't want to get caught getting drunk in his shed shouting stupid names.

That sobered them up quickly and they vowed to

come back next week and get serious about this naming thing.

Two Weeks Ago
Rachel was at the shed first. She was looking out for Sonia, hoping she'd come along before Mina arrived. Sonia did. She looked terrible, like she was wasting away. Rachel'd been noticing this, and decided to do a one-person intervention.

She sat Sonia down and began. "There's this formula in chemistry, Sonia, it's called the Cooling Curve of Napthelene."

"That's...what?"

"Shut up and listen. In chemistry, the cooling curve is a line graph that represents the change of phase of matter, typically from a gas to a solid or a liquid to a solid. And napthalene is a poisonous solid that can melt, like ice."

"So what? This's boring, girl." Sonia started to stand up and leave but Rachel stopped her by gently pushing her down. Just then Mina entered the shed. She had enough street smarts to know that something was seriously up and chose to sit on the floor in a corner and keep quiet.

"So what's happening to you is like not unlike that cooling curve. Your body is the napthalene, a solid. When you change the amount of energy you put into it, food, you start to melt. You loose a bunch of weight. And then you plateau. You quit melting and go solid again."

"Yeah. That's what I've done. Hit a plateau."

"No," said Mina sadly from her corner. "You've hit a bunch of plateau, girl, and you know it. You're melting faster than you're being solider. If that's a word."

Sonia took offence. "You're supposed to be my friends. Help me out, so's I can loose enough weight so Jimmy will love me again. But you're just turning on me. You're jealous because you're both still fatties."

"We're trying to help you out, Sonia," Rachel said. "We don't want you to disappear."

"Like she said," Mina said.

"Fuck you," Sonia said as she struggled to get up and walk a straight line out of the shed.

Today

Rachel and Mina meet at the shed. Rachel has the usual bottle of vodka and Mina has a huge bouquet of mixed white flowers in her arms.

"I thought Jimmy might've come."

"Ah, he's an idiot. She's well shut of him."

"She's well shut of everything, now."

"I've had an idea.

"Let's have it."

"Let's call ourselves, The Cooling Curve of Napthalene, as a memorial, sort of."

"No. That'd be too sad. Let's call ourselves, Cool Curves."

They high five.

"But where're we gonna find another red-headed French horn player as good as Sonia?"

"We'll find one. And she'd better be fat."

The girls put their arms around each other's shoulders, raise the vodka bottle, and take turns drinking memories of their lost friend.

Walking Through a Wrong Door

"Oh, Henry, it's perfect!" Glenda's enthused.

"You're right, hon, you're so right! It's so us!"

Henry and Glenda, standing side by side, arms wrapped around each other's waists, beamed their approval at the house agent. She, rather desperate to sell this house, but not wanting this trendy, newly wed couple to feel or sense her desperation, merely said,

"So glad you like it." She added, "This one's just come back on the market, and the price is a steal. Shall we step inside?"

She motioned the couple through the front door, but Henry swung Glenda up in his arms, and as he crossed the threshold with his new wife in his arms, said,

"This is our best door, hon, isn't it?"

"The best EVer," Glenda said with girlish glee. "Best EVer door! The ABsoLUTE right one!"

Once inside, all three moved across the marquetry floor to the floor-to-ceiling glass French doors, stepped out to where a trim-cut lawn extended beyond paving stones until it was stopped by a horseshoe of cedar trees, ancient guardians of the property called 43 Wisdom Lane.

Glenda clapped her hands in wonder.

"Oh, Henry, look at the cedars! Aren't they wonderful? Sort of cradelling us like!"

"You're so right, hon, cradelling."

Henry turned to the agent and said, "We'll take it."

The agent handed Henry the keys, saying as she did so, "Hope you'll both be very happy here," slung the couple a quick smile, and hurried away down the lane. Once back at her car, she climbed in, wiped her forehead with a dramatic, "Whew!", started the engine, and drove away, thinking, "I'll surely get agent of the month, maybe even the year, moving that great white elephant off the books."

Back at the house, the couple were exploring. "All this space!" Glenda exclaimed more than once. "All those trees!" Henry marvelled.

Glenda stared at the trees and said, "You know, I think I'd like you to thin them out, get more light in out there, hon. So we could have picnics in our forest."

"Your wish is my command," Henry said. "Put it on the list. Thin out Cedars."

The canvassing of their new house complete, the couple got down to the business of moving in and setting up house.

They brought in furniture, stocked the kitchen with the latest in gear and tools, filled the airing cupboards with linens and the pantry with storable food stuffs, loaded up the fridge and freezer, put up curtains and shades and generally had themselves a fine time. Together they spent an afternoon cutting down a few young trees to make an open, circular space.

"Look, hon," Glenda remarked once they'd finished, "there's another circle over there where someone must've thinned out some other trees."

"Great minds thinking alike, hon," Henry said.

One day, about a month after they'd moved in, Glenda was in the kitchen preparing a meal. She happened to look out the wide kitchen window and a bizarre thought crossed her mind. She called out to Henry, who was connecting up their entertainment center. "Hon? Come here a sec?"

Henry came. "What's up, cutie pie?"

"Well, call me crazy, but I think the lawn's gotten smaller. Look."

Glenda pointed out to their back garden. Henry stared at the space and shook his head.

"I'm gonna call you crazy, hon. It's just the same size it's always been! Now, come and see how I've linked up our computers and the TV/DVD player."

A few days later, Henry told Glenda he wanted to start a kitchen garden. Dig out a plot, plant yummy veges, maybe even a flower or two. Glenda loved the idea and joined him on Saturday.

Sitting back on her heels, watching her husband mark off a plot with string and small wooden stakes, Glenda gazed around her. With intense satisfaction. And then with the sort of faint alarm that furrows the eyebrows.

"Hon," she said, "it's happening again. It's getting smaller."

Henry, ever the patient newlywed husband, tried to smooth his wife's concerns. But to no avail. Finally, in an attempt to make things all better and get on with his marking out, he said,

"Look, hon, to ease your mind I'm gonna take some of this string and pull it from here," he indicated the edge of the paving stones, "to over there," pointing towards the center of the horseshoe of trees. "Then you'll see, it's just an optical illusion. Something about the light up here or something. Nothing to worry about. Okay?"

Glenda could never refuse Henry anything. Even though she was worried, spooked a bit, she said, "Okay, hon. Whatever you say."

The lawn fully marked off for a vege and flower garden and a string marker heading off into the trees, Henry and Glenda continued their life.

One afternoon, Glenda came home with a hilarious story. She'd been out shopping at their local supermarket, got caught short, ran into the hallway containing restrooms, went into a stall to do her business, noticed the seat up which she thought was a fine courtesy as she never sat on public toilet seats, finished up, walked out, and saw a man standing at the sinks, washing his hands.

"I'd been walking through a wrong door! "she said.

"To the men's, not the women's room!"

Henry loved that story. "You and your wrong doors, hon," he said. "Do you remember the time you walked through a door you thought led upstairs but it led down and you fell and nearly broke your head open? That was a hoot!"

"It hurt," Glenda said with a smile, "but not as much as my pride. Honestly. You'd think I'd learn how to walk through doors by now. But wait a minute. You do it just as much as I do! What about the time I found you walking through a wrong door into the neighbor's house, when we lived downtown?"

"Well, that was a mistake anyone could make. All those doors looked the same, didn't they. Come on, hon, didn't they?"

Glenda hugged her husband: "Of course they did, hon. And now," she cast a proprietarial look around her, "we've definitely walked through the right door into this house. No more wrong doors for us!"

Two days later Henry went out to water the seeds he'd planted. He happened to glance outwards towards the trees. Could it be? Was there less string between him and them? He walked out to the perimeter and there, sure enough, was proof positive.

His string vanished into the forest, no longer pegged out at the edge of it.

Still, he thought nothing more about it until a week later when Glenda came into the house screaming. "It's happening! The trees are moving! I can't stand it! We have to move, get out of here, before they get us!"

Henry went and stood at the French doors. Sure enough, there was half the lawn left. The trees were definitely closer.

Now, not being of a scientific bent or overly curious, that night the pair decided to go to bed, have a good sleep, and decide what to do in the morning. Always best to decide in the morning.

Two weeks later, the agent was standing with Minnie and Stan in the empty house. "What do you think?" she asked. "This one's just come back on the market, and the price is a steal."

Minnie rushed over to the French doors and, looking out, said to Stan, "Oh, baby, look at all those lovely trees!"

Stan looked and appreciated, but he didn't know what they were called. He turned to the agent and asked her.

She said, "They're Western Cedars and you mustn't try to thin them out. If you do, they will not like it."

Who is Willing

There was never enough food at Sasha's house. Sometimes she had old bread for breakfast, had to steal from trash cans for her lunch, and supper might be thin soup made from a cabbage leaf. So Sasha was always hungry.

One day Sasha found almost a whole meat loaf in a dumpster. She was so excited, she grabbed it up and ran all the way home. Her new father caught her up as she bounded up the cement lawn. He smelled bad and held her too tight. The meat loaf fell from her arms.

Sasha's new father laughed and stepped on the meat loaf, grinding it into a mushy mess.

That night Sasha stole all the money in the cookie jar, which wasn't much, threw some clothes into one of her lost brother's backpacks, and ran away.

With almost all of her money, Sasha bought a bus ticket to a town a hundred miles away. As the bus pulled out of the station, Sasha didn't even think of looking backwards. She was excited to imagine trying on herself in a new town, maybe lying about her age, getting a job in a cafeteria so she'd never be hungry again, maybe finding a best friend.

But the bus never got to that other town.

It broke down in the middle of the prairie wilderness. Many people on the bus panicked; some pasted worried looks on their faces, got out their cell phones; some even stood by the side of the road expectantly. Some were brave enough to stick out their thumbs and hitch a ride. Soon, everyone was gone except Sasha and the driver. He looked her over with a look she'd seen before on her new father's face, so she took off running.

She ran for a while, and then noticed the landscape around her. It was open and free. She was open and free. No one in the way. No one to look at her like the bus driver, no one to scold her like her mother did over nothing, no one to stop her from taking the last morsel of food on the table. Sasha had that thought and then knew she was hungry. She set out to find food for herself in this new, wild, open, free place.

The first thing she did was find a big rock to sit on.

The second thing she did was close her eyes.

Then she wondered how she'd find wood for a fire. She'd need a fire if she found food, that much she knew. And water. She'd need to find water, she thought.

The third thing she did was imagine a rabbit coming to sit by her. The next thing she did was imagine the rabbit offering itself up to her for food.

Soon Sasha grew bored sitting and thinking and wondering, so she got up and started looking for wood. She found what she thought would be enough sticks and brought them back to her rock. She was beginning to think of this rock as a home base. She dumped the sticks on the ground and sat on her rock. How was she supposed to make fire out of a bunch of sticks?

While she was trying to figure this out, she thought she heard a light crunching sound behind her. Trying to stay cool and collected, to act as if she knew exactly what she was doing, she turned her head. There, standing as if growing up out of the wild, open, free prairie wilderness, was a boy who looked so much like herself that Sasha thought she was looking in a mirror. A tall mirror, out here in the open and free.

Without a thought as to why a mirror should be out in the wild, open, free prairie wilderness, Sasha opened her mouth and out came a rolling laugh. It started small, like a shore break wave, then built itself up into a righteous hang-10 wave and flung itself out toward the mirror Sasha boy.

The mirror shattered. Yet the boy still stood, quietly, calm, hands loose at his sides, his whole being relaxed. As if waiting.

"We are Willing," he said.

Sasha immediately felt calmed by his voice and still manner.

"Who is willing?" she asked.

"We've been waiting for you."

Sasha shuffled her feet back a few steps; too much was happening too fast and it frightened her even though the boy had about him a sense of safety that waved towards her. She held out one hand, as if to say, okay.

The boy turned and started to walk deeper into the prairie wilderness. Sasha found herself following, somewhat scared, mostly hungry.

"Is there food where we're going?" she asked the back of the boy as he steadily walked on.

"There's everything where we're going," he replied, turning his head as he said it.

In what seemed to Sasha like a flash of lightning, they were standing in a tall tree-surrounded circle. Inside the outer circle there were many others like the Sasha boy, some older, some younger. All standing quite still.

Inside their circle was a circlet of flowers of every description, flowers so bright and colorful Sasha felt almost blinded by their beauty.

Inside the flower circlet was a circle of stones around a dirt ground. And, in the center of this ground, was a small bowl.

Even though Sasha's mother had told her time and time again not to stare, she couldn't help herself. First at the trees, then the people, the flowers, the bowl. The bowl beckoned her. It seemed to her to be made of some kind of metal because it shone. Like the sun shines on a cloudless day.

Two of the people came toward Sasha; one took a hand and led her forward, into the circle, the other picked up the bowl. This was passed from person to person, who first picked a flower and then put it in the bowl. As the bowl passed, and more flowers added to it, Sasha was sure the bowl would overflow. It did not. The bowl came to her last. She looked.

Inside the bowl was all the food Sasha had been craving all her life—fruits and vegetables and milk and meat and kisses and hugs and songs and dances and lots and lots and lots of chocolate. She couldn't believe her eyes, but her tongue and stomach began to taste and feel the food, her skin tremble from touch, her feet itched to move. She opened her mouth and a song came out, the most beautiful song she'd ever heard but didn't know she knew.

All of the people joined her in the song and when it came to an end, they all sat down. A soft, subtle hum filled the air above and around the circle.

"I am Hope," said the smallest.

"I am Courage," said the oldest.

"I am What," "I am When," "I am Why," "I am Where," said a group sitting next each other.

Finally, the Sasha boy from the mirror said, "And I am Who."

Everyone stood up again, linking arms around waists, forming a never-ending circle.

The very eldest said, "We are Willing. We are willing to try, willing to believe, willing to start over; we are willing to move beyond fear into joy. Who is Willing, What is Willing, Where is Willing, Hope is Willing, Why is Willing, Courage is Willing, and When is Willing. We all are willing." The eldest looked at Sasha. "Are you willing?"

Sasha opened her mouth to speak, to ask a question that was forming along the channels of her mind, but instead of speaking, she found herself suddenly whooshed up in the air and swept along in a current that moved faster, ever faster. With a soft bump, she landed. Back in the world she'd run away from.

When, many years later, Sasha died peacefully in her sleep, people came from all over the world to say goodbye to her and to celebrate her long and prosperous life.

They honored her courage, her willingness to try, to push against the odds when her life had become almost unbearable in those early years.

They recalled the books she wrote about a fantasy people named Willing who lived out on the prairies, one book a year for fifty years. What an accomplishment.

They rejoiced in her personal and professional successes with the schools for orphaned girls and boys she'd opened.

But most of all, they remembered her with love. With a dance. With a song. With laughter. With hugs and kisses. With a feast to please even the fussiest of the gods and goddesses. And with lots and lots and lots of chocolate.

THE END

Lightning Source UK Ltd.
Milton Keynes UK
UKHW020836081019
351208UK00006B/248/P